BRIGHT NEON FUTURES

A WHOLESOME CYBERPUNK ANTHOLOGY

Published by
Edward Caio

Editors: Edward Caio, H.M. Simmons, and Angelica Curzi

ISBN: 9798563990104

Cover design © Luana Vecchio / www.luanavecchioart.com

Typesetting by Angelica Curzi / Twitter: @AngelicaCurzi

BRIGHT NEON FUTURES

EDITED BY
EDWARD CAIO • H. M. SIMMONS • ANGELICA CURZI

TABLE OF CONTENTS_

>entry #1

>entry name:

BACK IN MY DAY

>

>

>entry author: EDWARD CAIO

>

>

>access author info

>Edward Caio is a writer and part-time anthologis currently based in Italy. After producing Dar Destinations: *An Anthology of Terror* and *Oscurità: A Dar Anthology*, he thought it might be fun to do something little bit different. He stands by his opinion that Roy wa the true protagonist of Blade Runner.

>Tweets and Instagram: @tedwardcaio

>show entry_

Lucy's favourite days were Sundays, because that was when her grandad would come over for lunch, and they would cover an encyclopaedia's worth of topics, so natural was their conversation. One such Sunday she decided to share her latest idea: they should start a podcast.

"A podcast!" he said, chuckling as he helped set the table. "Does your generation even listen to them anymore?"

"I suppose not," she said. "We listen to taps now."

"Taps?" he asked, furrowing his brow in confusion.

"Like podcasts, but shorter and more frequent, like drops from a tap."

"How much shorter?"

"About a minute long, two for big episodes."

"A minute? Just one minute? That's barely enough time for anything!"

"No it's not, it's the perfect amount of listening time! A minute of history or science or an interview before work, or before bed, it fits into the modern daily schedule."

"In my day, a podcast was much much longer, about one or two hours, not minutes!" She looked up, positively shocked by this.

"That's so long! When would you find the time to listen to it?"

"You just find it! While cleaning the house or playing videogames, or on your commute..." She gave him a quick look and was about to say something, before he rolled his eyes. "Most people had to commute to work in those days and we had to find something to do, it wasn't always a remote work deal."

"But didn't you start working remotely full time when you were twenty-two, too?"

"If the video call software worked! My internet was reliably unreliable, sometimes I had to venture around town, asking if I could please use the free WiFi, which was obviously never free because it was for customers only. I had to set up in the corner and pretend I was at home, or in an office space. Thank goodness I never got caught. Nowadays you get perfect connection anywhere, you don't even have to think about it."

"I hate to sound like a cliche, but I don't know how you survived like that," she said, passing him the napkins.

"Neither do I when I really think about it," he said. "As a backup I could always use my phone as a hotspot with 4G and—"

"4G!" she exclaimed.

"Yeah, why?"

"That must have been incredibly slow!"

"Luce, I'm just old enough to remember the end of dial-up, you don't wanna know what slow actually looked like."

"Still, 4G isn't exactly 36G."

"Gs, schmees, I can't even tell the difference from one G to another anymore, it's all much too fast. You don't learn the art of patience." He always accompanied his teasing with a light smile. Lucy was a very bright girl with a lot of patience for a sixteen-year-old, but playfully scolding her for occasionally adopting her friends habits was another fun Sunday pastime.

"I learn it by dealing with you!"

"Yes, and you unlearn it by watching the latest blockbusters."

"Gramps please, spare me the movie argument!"

"Dad, please!" said Lucy's mother, coming in with the meat and potatoes. "Otherwise I'll have to send you back home, and I can't possibly finish today's lunch by myself!"

"But I'm right! Films nowadays, they have no structure, no character, it's all filters and effects and men with fancy jawlines!"

"Hollywood actors have always been stupidly hot!"

"And now they're even more hot, it's ridiculous! Everyone looks like the lovechild of Henry Cavill and Chris Evans! Now there was a real movie star that Evans, I remember being just eighteen when I saw *Avengers: Infinity War* at the cinema, *that*'s a bonafide Hollywood classic for the ages there! And!" he said, excitedly raising his finger, "we had to wait a whole *year* before we got to see how it ended! How's that for patience?" She tried not to laugh as she rolled her eyes. "We had art cinema too. Pretentious as hell, but a lot of fun. Unless you were at uni and lived with a film student, then you learned to curse God for creating art cinema. But it was fun and different and experimental, real food for thought. Now every movie and every show is controlled by a rodent. So terribly sad."

"In this family we stan the rodent!" said Lucy.

"Where'd you learn that?"

"Stan?"

"I've not heard that term in eons!" he said, chuckling to himself. It was one of those words he started using 'ironically', before it naturally fell into his everyday lexicon. Like every other slang word he learned.

"By watching old-timey movies," she said, smugly. "I'm more of a connoisseur than I let on!"

"That's my girl," he said.

"I always try and imagine you back then, with your phone and old e-reader, your 2010's style and earphones with wires, gasp," she said, holding her hands to her cheeks in fake shock.

"Those were already a relic when I reached your age, I'm just stubborn. I made fun of the other kids for losing their airpods."

"How do you even lose those things, they're huge!"

"Why, how small are yours now?" he asked.

"I'm wearing them right now." He double-took, eyes wide.

"You're joking!" She shook her head, smiling at his reaction. He leaned in to inspect her ears, empty as his. She reached in with both thumbs and forefingers, pulling out two minuscule, semi-transparent plastic earbuds, both half the size of her pinky nail. He picked one up to inspect it.

"Everything shrinks..." he whispered to himself. He handed it back.

"You want a pair?" she asked, sincere.

"Puah! What would I listen to with them? All music sounds the same these days!"

"Oh dad, sit down and eat!"

"We had Kendrick, we had Lady Gaga, we had Drake, we had Post Malone!"

"Ooh, Post Malone," said Lucy. "I like him, he's good."

"And we had to have our phones charged and our headphones connected via bluetooth to appreciate them, no head-streaming!"

"It seems like a lot of effort went into setting up just to listen to a song."

"Maybe," he said, reflecting. "But I tell you, we really did put more effort into a lot of things, everything had to be done with intent!" He emphasised that last word, knowing he sounded a bit ridiculous. "Even on the socials, you can get famous over literally a night. In my time, you had to grind for your clout!"

"As if fame has never been just a game of luck!" said his daughter, patiently waiting at the table, but enjoying her father's rambling too much to interrupt.

"My buddy at school, I tell you, he started vlogging at fifteen, he finally broke half a million subscribers at eighteen," he said.

"The movies always make out that everyone was vlogging even back then, was it like that?" asked Lucy.

"Sure thing, there was a boom when I was a teen. Soon they were becoming mainstream, the new rockstars, and everyone wanted to try it. It's why everything you own now has a video camera. But back then these poor guys had to lug their equipment around and risk their dignity in the process, plus they had to carry their batteries and SD cards, and so on and so forth. Even stories took effort. Nowadays you don't even have to think to edit a small video, and it shows!" He began to take his seat at the table, and shot Lucy a quick look. She had a face like she was on to something, and it worried him just a bit.

"I have a question."

"Sure."

"Did you, uh... ever try your hand at vlogging?"

Grandpa turned to his daughter. "Darling, would you kindly pass the potatoes?"

Another thing he noticed on that wintery afternoon, as he was walking down the beach with Lucy, was that oil rigs were now wider and taller than they used to be. And they used to be far out in the middle of the ocean, not lined up just an odd twenty miles from the shore, in plain view. The view used to be cleaner, emptier. So much more sky. Hell, he remembered when billionaires paid heavily to have wind farms removed to avoid 'spoiling the view'. Maybe, he thought, they weren't really all that concerned with the view after all.

"I was wondering," said Lucy. "Is there anything you do like about the present?" He laughed.

"They invented better ways of storing pictures of the past." She found that funny too. "I joke," he said. He took a second to think, reflexively rubbing his chin, another habit she liked to tease him for on occasion. This time however, she watched and waited.

"Well," he said. "I talk a lot about patience, but I don't miss the days when you'd only get one bus every half an hour, or a train every ten minutes. If you missed it, your whole day was in ruins. Then again, if you got on during the summer the heat itself could mess you up for the day too, especially on the metro. Thank goodness for improved schedules and competent air conditioning." He scratched his nose before continuing. "Mail is improved, which is something I never thought would happen. I hated waiting for mail, too much anxiety. I can't tell you how happy I was when NewPost was founded, five days turns into five minutes. I literally ordered so much stuff just so I could make the most of it!" Lucy laughed.

"You're such a geek!"

"One day you'll learn to appreciate the little things too, then we'll see who the geek is." He paused for a second. "It'll still be me, let's be honest. I mean, I remember when they finally got round to commercially available space tourism. They had talked about it for ages, and when it finally opened I had to wait at least another ten years to get a place. But that day when I got on, they played the safety video and all, and the craft looked incredibly clean, very deliberately futuristic. I was so excited. Then they launched us, straight up through the atmosphere. I still remember watching the sky turn from that soft blue into pitch black. I really had never felt anything like that. And for the record, flat-earthers have been rather quiet since space tourism started."

"Which company did you fly with?"

"There was a major company that got there first, but BlackStar Aviation set up shop shortly after."

"I've flown with them too!"

"When?"

"When I was twelve," said Lucy. "To be honest, it was fun but... I thought it was fine. Nothing special. I don't know if I got the appeal."

"You couldn't. You've been robbed of that. When you've grown up with space travel as an ambition rather than as a choice, you'll never feel the thrill of reaching that." He paused to think. "Unless they invent time travel in your lifetime, then perhaps you might."

"It's true though. I can't imagine that thrill."

"I've always loved a good thrill. Which reminds me," he said, pointing his finger up as if to make a point once more. "Rollercoasters. They've gotten so much better. Bigger drops, faster speeds, better designs, and more importantly, they're much much safer! Have you been at Seventh Run recently?"

"I'm not really much of a theme park person."

"This is the one crucial thing your mother didn't inherit from me. Try the Mach Steel at Seventh Run, then come back and say you're not a theme park person! Barrels of fun, I'm telling you."

Laughing, she asked "I thought you liked the quiet life, like other old people."

"Eighty-six is not old, I beg your pardon." He stopped, hit by a sudden moment of reflection. "Not anymore," he admitted. Lucy perceived the subtle shift in tone.

"Is everything alright?"

"It really is, in a sense," he said. "It's odd. When I was your age, healthcare wasn't as refined as it is now. It was fine, but unfortunately more hit and miss than it should have been at that point. Now I'm eighty-six, feeling as fit as forty. If I was eighty-six in twenty sixteen, i'd need a walking stick. My final days would be round the corner." He let out a small chuckle.

"I suppose I couldn't go on rollercoasters either. Not that that would stop me trying." Lucy smiled. He continued. "I do still remember. It had it's holes in the system, and it wasn't completely accessible either. A real mess for some. Thankfully rather than a common cold they soon caught common sense, and so they got that sorted too."

"Talking to you always gives me perspective. I don't think I'll ever grasp how much has changed," she scoffed.

"I think what you'll have a harder time grasping is how much hasn't changed."

"Such as?"

"Well, we've made progress, but politics is always the same game. It's less about ideas to help people and more about playing chess so you can gain a few millimetres. The 'debate' keeps raging, but it's always the same talking points, reheated for a new age. We never got anywhere really in fighting climate change, for example." He pointed at the waves, gently crashing onto the shore. "The water used to be much lower, there used to be a large pier over there, but it had to be dismantled for security concerns. Huge pity. Unfortunately, people refuse to listen to long-established truths and make their own instead."

"As if you've never done that," said Lucy, smiling coyly. He smiled and wagged a finger at her. Touché. He'd raised his daughter well, who in turn raised Lucy even better.

"I guess some things never do change. Call it the good old human condition." He cleared his throat before continuing. "Such as old men complaining about the past." She chuckled. But after that she was quiet. They walked along the beach for a good few minutes before he decided to ask.

"What's eating you?" She kept her gaze down towards the sand as they kept strolling.

"I guess... I really am surprised. Sitting in the virtual classrooms, one gets the idea that through history, humanity kept moving forward. I suppose it did in a way, but I hoped it would have kept doing so in a better direction. Instead we keep making bad decisions, stacked on the bad decisions that came before. How much more progress could we have made if we'd actually learnt from the past instead of throwing around quotes about learning from the past? It's just... so sad." They'd both stopped. She was still looking down at the sand. He placed a hand on her shoulder, prompting her to look up.

"I know what you mean. I know exactly what you mean. Because I've been there. And my parents have been there too. And their parents before them. Every generation gets to see artist's renditions of their utopian future, accompanied by reassuring claims of 'you have this to look forward to'. Then we find out that only ten percent of it becomes true, if we're lucky. But that's ten percent more than we had before. After that, we get ten percent more. Some generations aren't that lucky, they get five percent. Others are and might be luckier, and achieve fifteen percent. That's how it works. You aim for a hundred, and do the best you can. You fight for those crucial baby steps. And anything above zero is a victory. That's why young people should always learn patience. Because it sure isn't going to get any faster." Lucy smiled, and hugged him, and he returned the embrace.

"I bet I sounded really cool saying all of that," he said.

"It was very good."

"You want to get ice cream?" He felt her chin bobbing on his shoulder. He let go and started walking. "I know a place just here." He lead the way, and she enthusiastically followed. "Wait until I tell you about ice cream trucks. If I had a time machine..."

She laughed out loud and told him to stop. But she listened anyway.

>entry #2

>entry name:

THE EMULATING ANDROID

>entry author: PAUL CARROLL

>

>

>access author info

>Paul Carroll is a writer and comic creator from Dublir His work primarily focuses on the extraordinary. Hi current series, *The Black Pages*, focuses on a millennia Grim Reaper and a magical Detective. He is a foundin member of both Limit Break Comics and Cupán Fae Dublin-based creative groups.

Tweets: @writeranonymous | paulcarrollwriter.com

>show entry_

"All systems operating."

"Andy? Are you with us?"

Andy blinked, in as close to an approximation to blinking as he could manage. His eyes refocused, centring on Becky and Doug. They stared at him with expectation written across their faces. "I am with you, Becky," Andy replied. "Might I ask why I am restrained?"

Doug chuckled to himself. "Sorry, my bad." He released metal clasps around Andy's arms and waist. "There you go, buddy."

Andy took a tentative step forward. The clunk of metal on metal rang through the room. Andy knew it well. This was home, the laboratory of Becky Parker and Douglas Stuart. "You both look worried," Andy noted. "Is there something wrong with me? The last timestamp on my memory banks records events from several hours ago. I was offline for quite some time."

The doctors looked to each other and tried to relax. Andy could see their shoulders relax, but it did little to ease their heartbeats, or affect the dilation of their pupils. "Andy, declare Operation Emulator," Becky said to him.

Andy's freewill became restrained, much in the same way as his body had been just moments ago. Without hesitation, he announced, "Operation Emulator. Subject designation: Andy. Version 1.04. Phase: Beta. Purpose of operation: monitor the subject's capacity for emotion emulation." Andy's self-control returned. "I see. This is good news, isn't it? Why are you still worried? My diagnostics indicate that I am still functioning at full capacity."

The doctors shared another glance. "There was a power surge during the upload process," Doug explained. "We aren't sure what it might have done to the emulator. We're sure it's nothing. It'll be fine."

The problem with androids, particularly ones built like Andy, is that it is difficult to lie to them. The emulator that had been installed within him only made it easier to read expressions and emotions. He knew that Doug was worried that something might malfunction. He knew that Becky was biting her tongue—figuratively and literally—on the matter: her stress levels were higher than what humans deemed normal.

Still, Andy knew, humans lied to those they loved all the time. Beautiful lies to protect those closest to them. Andy's face could smile, but he was capable of hiding how he felt, at least on the surface. As Becky and Doug explained the field tests to him, he continued to analyse their expressions and ignored the artificial feeling of butterflies in his stomach.

The world was a strange and dangerous place for humanity. In the last couple of centuries, despite averting disaster on multiple fronts, people struggled with the reality of their planet. Andy was built into a world of artificial limbs as a result of war and disease, cybernetics designed to replicate authentic body parts. Pandemics were always a worry. The last outbreak, barely a decade ago, had crippled the medical staff that fought on the frontline to keep people alive.

That was when funding into the development of androids began. Andy was part of a newer line, complete with synthetic skin and eyes that could blink. His feet still clinked on the ground and the sounds of mechanical systems whirring through him could be heard if he ever exerted himself. It wasn't an oversight in design. People wanted to know who was human and who was android, built to serve.

Becky once explained to him that he wasn't a slave or an object, but that he was needed to help. He was necessary. "You're going to be a doctor, Andy," she had told him.

"Like you?" he had asked.

"No, Andy. Not like me. Doug and I, we're not medical doctors. We're the sort that experiments and programs. We're the type who try to fix the way the planet works, instead of fixing people."

Out of that came the emulator. Andy was their subject and he would have patients. The problem, of course, was that people *liked* having human doctors. They wanted someone with a bedside manner. They wanted a genuinely warm smile and for someone to understand that their pain wasn't just physical. They wanted a doctor who could empathise when they gave bad news.

Training doctors, though, took too long. Many were now surviving through Iron Lungs, cybernetic transplants that took a heavy toll on their ability to work the way they used to.

Andy knew all of this. It had been shown to him, either by upload or by direct sensory demonstration, in much the same way as he knew how to perform surgery or diagnose an illness. It was why, a couple of days after the installation of the emotion emulator, Andy stood in the middle of a park in London with Doug and Becky, both wearing protective masks and clothing.

"Initiate Emulator Training Protocols," Doug stated. A chime sounded from Andy's head.

"Okay Andy, this is your time to shine," Becky told him. "Observe. Learn. This field test is to determine whether you're capable of emotion in the same way as humans. No one is aware that you are monitoring behaviour and actions. Do you understand? You'll be witnessing people in their natural environments."

"It's the only way we can be sure that the emulator won't alter your behaviour when you're placed in a professional environment. Humankind needs you to make medical treatment safer. People need a doctor who won't perish alongside them, but also one who understands everything they're going through. We know you won't let us down, buddy."

They left Andy to his own devices after that. London was a big city and even after climate challenges, political nightmares, pandemics, war, terrorism and periods of civil unrest, there was no shortage of people for Andy to navigate through. The old Underground was off limits for androids, in order to keep the space free for humans to get around the city, but there was nothing to stop him observing people as they entered the station.

He had never been allowed out by himself like this before. A rush of excitement washed over him, causing his hands to shudder for a moment before he understood what was happening. "So that's what Doug and Becky feel," he noted aloud. He marched through the station, his feet clanking against the ground. He didn't know where he was. He could have checked, but there was a thrill about not knowing that he dared to test within himself.

Androids were typically monitored. It was how it had always been. People were paranoid around them, given the wealth of science fiction films and books that existed about android uprisings. It was how Andy had been given an understanding of Asimov's laws of robotics, which had been used as a guideline for his programming.

He stood by a pillar, watching people figure out which way they needed to go, which platform would suit them best, who best to avoid as they hurried on their way. Andy watched them with curiosity that he had never known before, a sense of what he logged internally as wonder welling inside him. The emulator fed emotion through his circuits to mimic human sensations and he was sure if he was physically capable of crying, he would have. Instead, his eyes brightened, torches in the dark station under a dreary sky.

The android allowed himself to people-watch for a few minutes, until he was sure all he was going to witness was panic and unfettered rage. Andy wasn't sure what people did, in reality. Becky and Doug had allowed him to analyse human behaviour in the past, but general routines and historical data did little to inform him about how people *really* behaved when they weren't keeping track. With that in mind, he decided to wander. There was no better way to monitor human nature than when they were free from the rigid structures of economic and societal demands.

Andy was occasionally stopped by the police as he wandered London. They scanned his wrist, where his identity chip had been placed for ease of access. Every time, he was allowed to keep going: scientific experimentation had granted him freedom that no other android possessed. Still, people were suspicious. The application for Andy to explore the city was not readily granted and few people outside of the emergency services had legal access to the sort of technology that allowed them to scan IDs.

He found himself, at one point, by the Thames. The water was murky, in parts, but Andy was aware of the ecological projects in development to purify water around the world. Even though the city had been subjected to more than one catastrophe, tourists routinely made the trip to the capital for getaways. He sat on an empty bench, cognisant of anyone who might request him to vacate the space, and took up his role as observer once more.

Becky had once explained to him—in the time before his emulator—that romance was one way of displaying feelings of love. She had tried to give him examples of what might be considered romantic, but kept falling short. "Flowers," she had said, "aren't romantic in and of themselves. It's the gesture of giving them that counts."

Without much consideration for feelings, Andy had responded, "In that case, anything can be considered romantic and romance loses any meaning."

She hadn't known how to react.

Now, Andy thought he understood. As he sat on a bench by the Thames, next to the site of the old Tower of London, he was witness to a proposal. A man had gotten down on one knee, completely unexpectedly, and produced a ring of glimmering garnet. The man's partner welled up in tears, first in shock and then in joy. Andy could read the emotions on a biological level as clearly as if they were written across his face.

The couple kissed, to some applause. Andy joined in, feeling it was appropriate to celebrate with the people he had been observing. He made an internal log: humans appreciate surprises from those they love.

Andy had barely made it further into the city when his sensors detected that someone was in a heightened emotional state. He made a note to congratulate Becky and Doug on the sensitivity of the emulator, before attempting to observe from a safe distance. He stood out of the way of pedestrian traffic, tuning his audio sensors towards the sound of a crying woman. He could see her, even from a distance, leaning into an older man.

London had known many pains, but the wonders of modern medicine and the strict behaviour of many citizens meant that father-daughter relationships could continue even as the parents aged into their seventies. Andy felt a frown form on his face as he watched. They were indeed related, but something was amiss.

"It's not fair," the woman wailed.

"I know, sweetheart," her father muttered.

"She was always so good about going out. She always wore her mask. She always kept her distance. She was healthy and she exercised and she ate right. She didn't deserve to go like that."

The woman's father repeated his empty platitude. Andy could hear his heart breaking with every syllable from the woman's mouth. He could have scanned them more fully, using facial recognition software to uncover their identities, but he knew that the application for Andy's exploration around the city did not permit him to unlawfully identify people, for fear of exploitation by the android or anyone with access to his servers. Even reading a man's heartbeat was cutting things close, but Andy couldn't help himself. He noted the sensation as curiosity.

Still, even without looking up their identities, Andy could see what was happening.

"This is grief," Andy noted to himself. He made a note in his internal log, combined with biometric scans and a transcript of the overheard conversation: some people cry when they miss someone that they love and others break inside.

By late afternoon, the emulator had read biometric data for thousands of people that Andy had passed by. He had observed fleeting moments of joy while people explored clothes shops, a gentle peace as a couple exited a bookshop, excitement as crowds poured from matinee performances on the West End and melancholy as every one of them inevitably passed a homeless man, or a memorial statue, or a fundraising station for the NHS.

He made a note to vocalise to Becky and Doug about the depth of human emotions he had witnessed and experienced in his time in the field. They would be analysing the data for a week, at least, and asking him direct questions that he could not help but answer. He didn't mind the restrictions on his free will. If the day had taught him anything, it was that people did the most ridiculous things for those that they loved.

He stopped himself. "Curious." He decided it would not be worth mentioning, unless he was asked. Even androids had their secrets.

Besides, the field test was not yet complete. He had a few more hours to wander London and there was so much more for him to witness. He was thankful—not for the first time since the test began—that a distraction presented itself as an opportunity.

Andy had witnessed all sorts of emotional outbursts during the day. He had seen people shout at each other. He had seen violence, quickly stopped by local police. Now, he watched a man strike his partner across the face. Part of him wanted to interfere. He could practically feel the man's anger in his own circuits, but his core programming prevented him from causing harm to a human. A single strike did not meet the qualifications for interfering in the case of inaction causing more harm than good.

The matter was further confused in his head as he sensed immediate regret from the assailant. He hadn't seen that before.

"I'm sorry, I…"

"I should have kept my mouth shut," the man's partner mumbled, nursing their cheek.

"No. No, I was just frustrated. I didn't mean to hit you."

Andy didn't need the man to continue. If he had a tongue, he would have felt the words sitting there. "I lost control. I would never hurt you on purpose. I love you." He listened as the man apologised, again and again, and they seemed to make up quickly thereafter.

The android wasn't sure what lesson he could derive from the couple's spat.

"Jesus, Becky, this is too damn risky," Doug shouted. They didn't know Andy had returned. They couldn't hear him, yet, but he could hear Doug and Becky in their lab. He could sense Doug's anger. "Do you know what would happen if this got out? Do you have any idea what would happen to us?"

Andy heard a crash, and Becky yelped. The emulator whirred in his circuits and he burst into the room. "Don't hurt her," Andy announced, putting himself between Doug and Becky. He didn't know what to do next. No one in London ever stopped a fight, except the police. He decided to try improvisation. The day was all about learning experiences, after all. "I cannot allow you to do any harm to her, Doug. I heard you arguing. I could sense your anger."

Becky placed a hand on Andy's shoulder. His sensors told him she was calm. "It's okay, Andy. Doug didn't hurt me. He wouldn't."

"But people hurt those they love," Andy responded.

The doctors shared a worried glance. Doug breathed deeply, to calm himself. "We're going to have to address that little nugget later, but we weren't arguing. I was frustrated. Something... something went wrong. You never should have been allowed out today."

"I do not understand."

Becky crossed the room, to join Doug. "Sit down, Andy." The android complied, though he wasn't sure if it had been an order. He knew people were asked to sit before they received bad news. "The emulator was running at over capacity. We've completed the analysis of some of the data coming from you throughout the day and it's worrying. The application we submitted for your freedom of movement..."

"We didn't account for you experiencing human emotions so quickly," Doug concluded. "You were only meant to be on a test, but the emulator was learning. We think it was the power surge."

"Did you feel anything strange today, Andy?"

The android considered lying, but he knew they would be able to tell once they monitored his outgoing data. "I felt..." He stopped himself. "I do not know. I thought I understood love, but it is complicated. I thought it was an emotion, but it comes with emotions of its own." He looked at Becky longingly. "Please ask directly."

She frowned. "Andy, report: emotional inconsistencies on your part."

The android sat upright. "Subject designation: Andy. Internal logs indicate sensations of love."

"Expand," Becky said. "Love towards whom."

"Love towards the doctors Parker and Stuart."

"Thank you, Andy. As you were." The android relaxed. "We'll need to run some tests to fully understand what happened. But otherwise, just on the back of what we've seen so far? Andy, we think your observations could help people. You could help people."

Andy perked up. "Do you mean I can become a doctor now?"

Doug chuckled. "Andy, buddy, there's so much more to you than just being a doctor. Your code, the parts of it that don't love us anyway, is the next step in the production of a whole team of doctors. If the emulator can continue to learn how to respond to people's needs, we'll have done it. We'll have solved the issue of bedside manners."

"My manners are fine," Andy told him and smiled. He stood up quickly and pulled the doctors into a hug. "I believe this is how humans show affection when words will not suffice."

The doctors hid their smiles. "Oh, that's one way."

>entry #3

>entry name:

HEAVENHELL CITY

>

>

>entry author: ANDREA REYNELL

>

>

>access author info

>Andrea is an Irish writer previously featured in *Th* *City Voice Anthology 2019* for her fantasy WIP, *River* Her latest piece, 'Heavenhell City', is her first tim writing in the cyberpunk genre. One day she hopes t work in the publishing industry; until then she'll happil read and write.

>Tweets: @Andrea_Rey48
>Blogs: writingblogwithbitsandbobs

>show entry_

Heavenhell City could be a dream or one hell of a reality check.

Today it was a nightmare for Serena.

The funeral was a brief affair. There was no coffin, only an urn with Aunt Iliara's photo placed behind it. Cemeteries had long since filled up and cremation was now law. Iliara was placed in an alcove beside Serena's parents. Afterwards the small apartment she shared with her aunt was filled with laughter and the smell of cooking.

The silence was deafening when everyone left. Serena grabbed one of Iliara's scarfs and fell asleep hugging it.

And so, life continued.

Serena threw herself into her robotics work, both as a distraction and to make up for the money that no longer came from Iliara's sick leave payment.

Robotics was a synch, but the customers… not so much. They appeared with their money and, as the joke went, disappeared back into Heaven, the upper city where the elite lived. They were guarded by a group of bodyguards who were little more than glorified hitmen whom citizens of Hell had dubbed 'Grifters'.

Clearly the Gods above hated Serena, as she now found herself in trouble because of one of these customers. Her colleague and good friend Jae steered her to the manager's office while Mr Santiago, owner of the biggest chemical factory in the city, screamed after her.

"I want that bitch fired!"

"Don't turn back, don't argue with me." Jae cut her off as he saw her mouth opening. "I've heard from my friend in IT that they're looking for any excuse to fire someone." As they got in the door, he dropped his hands from her shoulders. "And unfortunately, this encounter has provided *Todd*," he said the name like a curse, "with the perfect reason to let you go. Take what's yours: you patented the Zebular, they can't legally keep it. Find a better job that treats you well." Jae handed her the patents in a folder. "Hide it."

She flicked through it, handing back certain documents to Jae. "I can't take the blueprints for the Optics, it's too obvious, but what I can do is…" She grabbed a pair of scissors and chopped her name off the blueprint. "…Get rid of anything they could use against me. Give me a spare folder."

Jae did as asked and hurriedly replaced the amended blueprint back in the drawer.

She tucked the folder into the back of her jeans and sat at the chair on the other side of Todd's desk. "But isn't it illegal to fire me without any warning?"

"Yes, but they know that you won't take it up against them. Even if you sue for wrongful termination, they can drag it out and bleed you dry."

Serena bounced her leg and her hands grew clammy.

"Asshats. Thanks for the heads-up Jae."

"No, I wish I could do more, I—"

"Jae, you've done all you can in your position." She made a shooing motion with her hands. "Now go, there's no point in both of us getting fired."

Jae left with a pained look on his face. Todd walked in and sat down at his desk.

"Unfortunately, we're going to have to let you go. We've had a complaint and you're not suitable for Robotech Company." Todd held his hands out in a what-can-I-do-about-it gesture. "You have an hour to collect your things."

Two months later, Serena sat in an office at Alltech. The interview had gone well and she was waiting on the manager to return from copying her details. The door handle turned and the manager handed back her ID card with a frown on her face.

"I'm afraid there's been some bad news and we won't be able to take you on. We can't risk being Blacklisted too."

Serena's mouth dried up. This had been her last chance to be able to pay rent. She had even tried all the supermarkets for a job.

The manager leaned forward and spoke in a hushed tone. "It honestly seems like you were just at the wrong place at the wrong time, so here, I'll show you this." She held out a sheet of paper that turned out to be Serena's CV. But now her old job description was stamped through with a red "Terminated" and slashed through with a black mark.

Blacklisted.

"I'm really sorry. I'd suggest applying to an unemployment scheme and wait until this all blows over."

Serena managed a weak smile. "I appreciate you letting me know when no one else would." She stood up and shook the manager's hand.

"Apply here again when you can, we'd be lucky to have you."

Outside, the sky was threatening a storm. She tapped on her comms to activate the menu. She swiped through to her e-comm account and sent the unemployment activation form that was sitting in her drafts. Thunder rolled in the distance and a splat of rain hit her face before she ran to take shelter from the sudden onslaught of a downpour.

The rain wasn't stopping anytime soon, so she took her chances by taking a shortcut into the market district. The Greasers ruled this area, but with the weather there was no sign of any of the leather-jacketed, tech people around. She never paid attention to the whole gang turf war thing. If they were nice to her and caused no ruckus, she had no problems.

Her home had a notice stuck to it. "Hells, why I can't I just catch a break?" She ripped it from her door and skimmed over the words.

"New Management... building a hotel... paid five hundred to move... leave by the thirteenth of next month.

"So, they're offering me money that wouldn't pay one month's rent here and haven't bothered to provide me with an alternative home?" Her comms vibrated to indicate a newly received e-comm. *Unemployment Denied.* Hells, those assholes couldn't let her have one thing.

The following weeks were spent putting everything but necessities into storage. It cost her more than she'd have liked, but she couldn't part with Iliara's things. An attempt at getting more money from the developers was denied. The thirteenth came and went. An eviction notice was slapped onto her door. She had to face her new reality.

Couchsurfing worked for a while, but she couldn't let herself stay with her friends longer than two days. Her one night at a hostel left her with half of her stuff stolen and a black eye. From then on, she took her chances on the streets.

One night, she tucked herself into the corner of a shop entrance and covered her head against the rain. In what felt like a few minutes later, a shuffling sound woke her. She looked to find a figure running off with a familiar bag. Her brain sluggishly caught up a few moments later and she gave chase. "Stop, thief!" She splashed through puddles before skidding and tripping, her palms and knees were scored red with gravel. No one came. Serena trudged back to her spot. The last of her money had been in there. Now she couldn't even eat.

The morning, I'll decide something then. Why do I feel so hot? I'm outside. She sank into a restless sleep.

The morning light invaded her little patch of dry. Her neck was sore from the angle she had been sleeping at.

"We're gonna have te move ya." spoke a gravelly voice. "I can get ya some hot food but can't do much more."

Serena opened her eyes to a familiar voice. "Cal, is that you?" Her vision swam but now she felt cold, too cold.

"Hells above! I'd recognize tha' face anywhere, Miss Robotics. Wha's happened?" He helped her up and caught her when her knees buckled. "I hadn't seen ya in ages and wanted te show ye the new—Oh Hells! Yer burning up. We're going te a place ya can rest."

Serena didn't reply; she had slipped into the darkness.

There was a murmur of voices and she caught snippets of a conversation.

"That's her? Hells, she's unlucky."

"Nah, she's a good 'un…"

She blinked, opened her eyes and found Cal sitting beside her grinning. He was the boss of the Greasers and although he was now balding and slightly beer bellied, he had never stopped wearing his leather jacket.

"Welcome back, Miss Robotics, ye were ou' a few days wi' a fever. Nasty un, so it was. Sit yerself up there an' we'll talk."

Reluctantly, she told him the whole story and Cal nodded along, asking all the appropriate questions.

"That's the worst dose of bad luck I've come across in a while. Santiago did something similar to Johnny, but we got him a fake ID. What do ya say we make a deal and you have a think on it?"

"I'll hear you out but won't promise anything."

"There's the Miss Robotics I know."

In the end she agreed to a deal. They'd get her a new identification card in return for her robotics expertise and she had to work for them for five years.

Her next days were spent in Cal's Robotics and Repairs Shop, tinkering with a metal hand to fix the sensors. She stayed out of the other gang members' way when she could and only offered nods in place of smiles when it was unavoidable. They were friendly enough, but sometimes that could be a cover for something else.

Jae was happy when she finally contacted him, as she had to change her comms too. She made him swear to secrecy not to tell his family about her being Blacklisted. Serena was invited to a family dinner where Jae's mum stuffed her full of excellent food. She hadn't realised how much she missed a family dynamic.

When she got back to her room, she smiled.

She was no longer at rock bottom.

Cal gave her a docket with a home repair request. "It'll be a nice bit o' money for ya."

It was her first time being sent to the Grifters for tech support. She climbed the hill to where the mansions were. The city changed from sprawling grey concrete and dirt to clean, glittering pavements and white limestone estates. Hells, the sun even seemed brighter up here. Serena felt very out of place in her leather jacket and worn boots as she trudged up to the security desk, showed her new ID and was shown around the back of a towering house. She was passed off to another black-clad, body-armoured man who showed her into a workshop.

"Boss wants you to fix his new tech before he tries it out." He pointed to a piece of equipment.

"Alright, I need your boss to sign a waiver please." The Grifter grunted in response, took the form and walked out the door.

That left Serena to look around the room at the various gadgets that seemed to be in a state of permanent disrepair from the amount of dust that had gathered. She approached the item to repair in question. It looked familiar. Hells, it was familiar: that was her design. Serena gritted her teeth as she examined it. They had yet to figure out that they needed a constant infusion of Chemical X from the Optics to the brain so the robotic eyes wouldn't be rejected. She had given up on the project the day before she was fired as it was too risky with the potential loss of sight involved.

The bodyguard-butler came back brandishing a signature on the form.

"I'm afraid I can't carry out any repairs here, so I won't be charging for payment. Tell your boss that *his design* is fine, but without Chemical X, the body will reject it, causing potential loss of sight." She took the form and started to walk out the door.

"Do it or you'll be sorry."

"Hey, there's no need for a threat here. I won't be taking payment."

Next thing she knew, she was pushed back into the workshop and the door was slammed in her face. *Of all the things.* She thumped on the door and twisted the handle. "Let me out, this is not what I agreed to."

A muffled reply came through the door. "Boss wants you to fit it to him today. He's on his way."

What in the seven hells? "That's a no. Did you not listen to what I said? It can't be done safely." Footsteps receded. *Who was this guy anyway?* She unfolded the form. Maurice Santiago. This guy again?

It was the last thing she wanted to do for him after he had destroyed her life. She looked around her. *No windows, Hells.*

She couldn't call the police, as having a fake ID was a criminal offence.

"Why me?" She muttered. "I hate asking for help."

She called Jae on her comms. No answer.

She called Cal. He immediately picked up.

"Miss Robotics, wha' an honour. Thought ye said it'd be a cold day in Hell before ye'd call me." His hologram grinned at his joke.

"No time for jokes, Cal. It's *him* and I'm locked in a room in his mansion with my design. He wants me to fit it to him, but it's not safe and it's not a repair like stated on the customer request form."

"What's the problem? Yer designs are the best."

She dropped her voice to a whisper. "Santiago."

"Hells, tha' guy has ruined enough lives already. Hang tight, I'm coming over."

The door opened and Santiago strode in. He clicked his fingers at her. "I'm on a tight schedule here; do your job and leave. Payment will be in your account if I deem your work has been satisfactory."

This guy just couldn't be a decent human being. She counted to ten before she answered.

"I'm afraid your information is incorrect. Firstly, I won't be taking any payment as this is not a repair. This *design of yours* needs a chemical that will cause loss of sight unless you have an infinite supply of it. I am not willing to be liable for this. Now, I need to leave as I cannot help you any further." Serena replied in a sickly-sweet voice.

"You will do this and—"

Serena cut him off. "You signed the form for a repair only. I cannot help you anymore. Please let me leave."

Mr Santiago was positively livid at this point.

A knock on the door interrupted the impending rage that was to follow.

"It's Mr DuBois here to see you, Sir."

"Show him in." He turned to Serena. "Now you'll get what's coming to you." He sneered.

Cal walked in the door. "Now, Mr Santiago, you've my utmost attention. Wha' seems te be the problem 'ere?"

"Your employee won't do the job i paid her for."

Cal's eyes flicked over to Serena, waiting for her answer.

"I've not received any form of payment. I informed Mr Santiago's bodyguard that since this is not a repair as originally requested, I would not be charging for my expertise. This item is unsafe for use and I will not be applying it to Mr Santiago's person."

Cal nodded and turned to Mr Santiago. He held out the form and tapped the signature on the end. "You Maurice Santiago?"

"Clearly." Serena had never seen his rage so suddenly subdued. She suddenly wondered what Cal was capable of.

"See 'ere, 'ere and 'ere?" Cal pointed to various points on the form. "Says tha' we're only providing a repair service. We are no' obliged to take on any work that we deem unsafe. So, 'ere's what's gonna happen, me an' this lovely employee of mine are gonna walk out of 'ere untouched. *And if ye don't let us leave in the next five minutes, I've let my boys know that's the signal.*" Cal raised his voice slightly. "So wha's it gonna be Mr Santiago?"

Maurice Santiago said nothing.

"Tha's wha' I thought." He nudged Serena to start walking.

The next morning, she woke up and went about her day as usual but had this uneasy feeling. Since Cal had come to her rescue, she had decided to make more of an effort with the rest of the gang. "Johnny, I'm going for coffee, you want any? I'm buying."

All six-foot-three of a leather jacketed, blond-haired guy straightened up and regarded her with amusement. "Has Miss Robotics finally had a change of heart?" His mouth quirked up into a crooked smile.

"It's not dinner, Johnny; coffee or not?" Serena tried to keep a straight face but failed.

Johnny grinned back at her. "I'll take an Americano. Be back in twenty, I'm trying this bad boy out." He patted the hunk of metal that was his latest experiment.

"You got it to work?"

"If it runs first time, you're buying dinner."

She raised an eyebrow at him. "If it doesn't, I get to suggest that design tweak, and you're buying *me* dinner."

"Deal."

She grinned the whole way to the coffee shop.

Suddenly, her peripheral vison caught a sudden movement from an alley she was passing by. She jerked her head around and sidestepped quickly. A blow caught her on her shoulder, and she stumbled. Her legs were then kicked out from under her and she fell, hitting her head on the wall.

Her hands were tied behind her. A nondescript black van was waiting for her and she was dragged towards it. She began to kick and scream. The hands that had been dragging her dropped her suddenly. She slammed to the ground once more. In the next moment, her hands were free. She slowly sat up to see Johnny with one Grifter in a headlock while he made a call on his comms. The van screeched away in a blizzard of dust.

Cal appeared with five more Greasers in tow. Two sprinted away on his orders and another helped Johnny manhandle the Grifter away. Cal approached Serena and helped her limp to the nearest medical centre. Fortunately, she wasn't concussed but had to stay in overnight. Cal sat chatting with her until he was called away.

"I'm leaving two of my best guys with ya standing guard outside. I'll take care of Santiago."

Johnny walked in, took Cal's place at the bedside and handed her a burrito.

"If you really didn't wanna go to dinner, you could've just said so. It's easier than getting kidnapped."

Serena snorted at that and unwrapped her burrito. "How did you get to me so quickly?" She took a bite of her food.

Johnny chuckled. "I thought of a really great noodle place that closes before we finished so I thought we'd take off early and I'd catch you on your way back."

Serena was quiet for a moment. "Do you think Cal will be able to do something about Santiago?"

Johnny smiled. "We take care of our own. Don't worry about it."

He left as soon as her eyes started drooping and promised that he'd be there when she got discharged.

A few mornings later Serena switched on the TV. The breaking news revealed that Santiago had been rushed to a hospital after a robotics incident and was waiting arrest for embezzlement and fraud. Robotech had gone under after several product recalls and was being sued over customers going blind.

Her comms dinged.

Family breakfast at Martha's @ 11.

She checked the time and snuggled back into her duvet.

The first real smile in a long time snuck up on her.

Heavenhell City could be a dream or one hell of a reality check.

Today, it felt like home.

>entry #4

>entry name:

DEFRAGMENTATION

>

>

>

>

>entry author: CHRIS DURSTON

>

>

>access author info

>Chris Durston published his first novel, *Each Littl Universe*, in April 2020 and hasn't looked back sinc By the time you read this, he hopes to have done man more things – check chrisdurston.com to find out wha he's up to and where you can read more of his work cyberpunk and otherwise. His other interests includ dogs, food, and video games.

>Tweets: @overthinkery1 | chrisdurston.com

>show entry_

"Is this worth getting killed for?"

Oracle asks the same question every run. They stick to their assigned role most of the time, warning me of dangers ahead or inbound datastorms, but they can never resist throwing doubt at me in the quiet moments.

"Ask me if I get killed," I tell them, making my way down a narrow alleyway lit by the neon purple signs of the abandoned storefronts. Their light reflects off the buildings: all tall, angular things of metal and glass. The only other light, as always, is the vague red-green glow of error messages branded across what used to be the sky. When they first pixellised the atmosphere, it was an array of logos and sponsor messages. These days, though, it's all just crash reports. "If I don't, it'll have been worth it. If I do, might have to reconsider."

I don't need to mutter the words aloud, but I do anyway. It's for the same reason I insist that Oracle talks to me by vibrating the implant inside my ear, creating a physically audible voice instead of beaming their thoughts straight into my mind: because interacting directly with another mind is *weird*. Having another person's consciousness in my head has its perks, though—with access to both my sense data and the streams of information filling every mote of air with billions of bits and bytes, they're like my own personal mission control in my brain.

"That's a terrible answer," their voice complains.

"You're supposed to be keeping an eye out, not cross-examining me."

"Oh, yeah. Interference matching Fragment signatures, moving right to left across your twelve o'clock in... three seconds."

I groan—quietly aloud and as loudly as I can inside my head—and tuck my body up against the wall of the alleyway.

"That is exactly why you're meant to be paying attention, Oracle."

"I don't like Oracle anymore."

"You only changed it last week."

"Yeah, it feels... I dunno, kitsch. Call me... *Spyhawk*."

"I don't want to."

I exhale, muscles twitching, itching to move.

"Stay where you are."

This is my least favourite kind of situation: can't go forward, can't wait for my pursuers to catch up either.

Not for the first time, I internally curse the Siblinghood. You'd think they'd be more willing to let me take a few bits and pieces, what with having the entire city to themselves. Everyone else was smart enough to move away after the Crash, but the Siblinghood saw it as their opportunity to monopolise the territory and stayed, claiming ownership of everything that was left. Everything in every monolithic megacorp tower: all the resources, all the medicines, all the food. And they are not fans of thieves.

What did they think was going to happen? That everyone would just let them keep it all? People need stuff; I'm good at getting my hands on stuff. Unfortunately, Siblinghood quartermasters tend to be both persistent and resourceful about getting said stuff back and ruthless to boot. Bad combination.

So here I am: vicious humans on my tail, an inhuman mass of corrupted data blocking the way forward. Great career choice, Eve.

Finally, after more of my lifetime than I'd like to waste:

"You're clear," says Spyhawk. That might be the worst name yet, but they'll doubtless be bored of it by next week, so I don't foresee having to put up with it for long.

"Thank you ever so much."

I continue down the alleyway, then take a right so as not to risk crossing paths with the Fragment. They're dumb, a kind of ghost: no real will of their own unless their instinct to attack kicks in, but they're just about the worst thing you could run into. The city's full of them now, wandering clouds made of congealed bits of human minds. The Crash ripped people's digitised brains apart, scattering them until they collected into little mushy puddles and solidified into walking, murderous software living only to find more information to corrupt—and what's got more information than a human brain?

I've survived encounters with them before—which is more than many can say, the artist formerly known as 'Oracle' included—but I know better than to assume I could do it again.

"What's in the package, anyway?" Spyhawk asks, ever-curious. Although they can see everything I can (unless I focus hard on not letting them), they can't function within the inner city where I make most of my pickups. Too risky, even when accessing only the most localised and immediately available datastreams; too open to corruption.

"Just neural solder."

"Boring. Worth getting killed for?"

"You already asked that."

I hop up a fire escape to the rooftops and check on the grey sphere inside my pouch. The shiny surface is beginning to tarnish. I don't have long: once removed from the solution it's kept in, neural solder's only good for a short time before it decays. A thin protective shell covers the important part, the liquid metal within, but exposure to the air has already started wearing that away. I should've grabbed a proper container, but trying not to get shot can be quite distracting.

"I don't remember anyone commissioning neural solder," Spyhawk muses. "Was I asleep?"

"Nobody commissioned it," I say. "Personal errand."

"I'd like to register that, if I'd had a vote about this, I'd have dissented."

"You don't have a vote."

"I think I *should*." Spyhawk sounds half-affronted, half-weary. "If you get written off, that's me in the Great Recycle Bin in the Cloud, same as you. Your decisions affect both of us."

I think about saying something to the effect of 'should have thought about that before you got your original body written off and had to use my brain as a server for your consciousness', but it wouldn't achieve anything. We've been over it too many times to count; it usually ends with Spyhawk smugly reminding me that I won't uninstall them. They know this because I couldn't help saving them, a complete stranger at the time, which apparently proves I'm a fundamentally good person. It's extremely irritating.

Instead, I just close my pouch again and flex the synthetic fingers of my left hand, checking that the servos and motors haven't seized up. All my mods were done after the Crash, of course, or they'd have meant the end of me when it happened, but post-Crash tech has a habit of running less smoothly than the hyper-integrated digital world we had before. Satisfied, I start moving again. The half-light from the dull red-green glow in the sky casts a grimy fuzz over everything.

"If it's a personal errand," Spyhawk ponders, vibrating softly inside my ear, "why are we heading away from home?"

"Please stop talking unless you have something useful to say," I mutter.

They're not wrong; our home, such as it is, is on the outskirts—closer to the skyscraper-sized routers where the Fragments concentrate than most people would want to live, but useful for work. We're heading beyond even the outskirts, to the settlements outside. Places that weren't digitised when the Crash happened. It's almost funny how that worked: everyone in the city was so desperately entwined in their electronic existence that when the inevitable breakdown happened, those who survived were the ones whom city society considered disadvantaged, backwards, unmodern.

I used to live out here, too, although I haven't told Spyhawk that. I don't know where they came from either, whether they survived the Crash because they already lived outside the city or because they didn't auto-install the fatal update and then managed to escape what came after. I'll ask eventually.

"You're gonna have to go down to street level," murmurs Spyhawk. I snap out of it, realising that I've been moving almost on autopilot while my thoughts dwelt on things there's no point dwelling on. "No more convenient rooftops after this next one."

It's not far now: we're leaving the sharp angles and

reflective surfaces of the city behind, approaching a place of achingly quaint houses made of old-fashioned bricks.

"Ugh."

"Hope you don't have much farther to go."

"It's fine," I say, not meaning it in the slightest. "Fragments don't come this far from the central routers."

"Well," says Spyhawk.

I stop moving. "What do you mean, *well*?"

"I mean they don't *usually* come out this far," Spyhawk says. "Although…" There's a moment of silence; I can *feel* Spyhawk's perception moving to scan the surrounding area, checking the signals from the stray datastreams all around. It's like something itching in my brain, trying to make a hole in my skull to peek out from. "Hm."

"What?"

"I'm not picking up bodies pursuing us anymore."

"Well, that's good."

"There's something…" Spyhawk pauses. "Can't tell what, but I'm getting something coming from the city."

"A transmission?"

"Feels like a Siblinghood signature, but I can't see where it's going or what it's doing."

"And it's moving in the same direction we are?"

Spyhawk considers this for a moment. I can almost feel them humming thoughtfully, a little vibration that isn't really there tickling at the base of my skull. "Seems that way."

"That can't be good," I mutter. My hand goes to the pouch and I sneak another glimpse at the little ball of solder. It's turning quicker than I'd hoped from shining chrome to a greenish-brown; I don't have long to get it where it needs to be. "Can't stop, though."

Spyhawk gives me the neural-aural equivalent of a shrug and a '*meh*'. "I hope we're getting paid well for this."

"Fragments don't come out this far," I repeat to myself, ignoring them.

"Not *usually*," Spyhawk appends again, extremely unnecessarily in my opinion.

I drop down to the street, landing as quietly as possible on the asphalt. There's even less light out here, since the advertisements in the sky were fewer and farther between over the places where nobody could afford to spend money on them. On the one hand, I won't be as easy to spot, but on the other, neither will anything coming after me. I take it slow as I advance around corners and between houses; even Spyhawk's silent for once, perhaps hiding behind a couch somewhere in my brain and peeking out between their fingers.

Then the Fragment shows up.

It doesn't make a sound, not in the usual sense. Sound usually means vibrations travelling through the air, into the ear. When a Fragment screams, it's a barrage of pure corrupted data ripping through your body, setting your insides and your senses aflame. They might be dumb most of the time, but when they come across something to corrupt, the bits of them that used to be human lash out in pain and fury. That's the worst thing about them, that they used to be human—not because it makes them smarter or stronger, but because they know what hurts.

Spyhawk's yelling something, I think, but the Fragment's transmission is battering the little implant in my skull and everything is a drilling, scraping, screeching wall of meaningless noise. The micromotors in my engineered left arm are oscillating and ripping; it's no less painful than if real muscles were spasming wildly, tearing themselves out of my body.

I'm on the floor, helpless; my right arm clutches at my head, left arm throwing itself around in useless, burning skitters. The Fragment comes towards me, I think—my only indication that anything's happening is more pain, harder vibrations. All my drivers are scrambling to make sense of the assault of shattered gigabytes.

Spyhawk's voice comes through, clearly, just for a moment.

"Overriding. Don't hate me."

Then there's a new pain, sharp and clean instead of the filthy burning, and I just about manage to lift my head enough to see my mechanical arm detach itself from my body. Spyhawk must have triggered the emergency eject, causing dozens of tiny blades inside the limb to sever every connection between muscle fibre and metal tissue before cauterizing each tiny wound. The arm slams its palm on the ground, launching itself towards the Fragment.

If the thing had a face, I think it might have looked surprised in the brief moment before the arm explodes, scattering the Fragment's body into thousands upon thousands of flickering bytes.

It disappears, torn to shreds. Before long, the data will ooze back to the nearest router and congeal into something like a humanoid shape again, but I'm safe for now. Minus an arm, but safe.

"Thanks," I croak. The sheer task of continuing to breathe through the pain has torn up my throat, but I'm alive.

"Welcome." Spyhawk doesn't have vocal cords, but their voice manages to sound exhaustedly relieved nonetheless. "Can I ask the question again now?"

"I'll tell you when."

I wobble the rest of the way to my destination, too tired to be cautious, just wandering down roads lined with brick houses in various states of disrepair and abandonment. When the one I'm looking for comes into view, I nearly collapse with relief; only the thought of the little ball in my pouch turning darker and darker with every passing moment forces me to keep moving until I make it to the front door. Spyhawk hums.

"*This* is it?"

"This is it."

The door cracks open a second later, and a young boy—unenhanced, just big dark eyes in a soft brown face—peers out. When he sees me, he flings the door open and dashes out, wrapping his arms around my waist.

"Auntie Eve!"

I put my one remaining hand on the doorframe, leaning heavily so I don't fall on him. I can hear Spyhawk wanting to ask, the telepathic equivalent of leaning forwards and tapping fingers on a table, but they stay quiet.

"What, you thought I'd forgotten?"

"No," Malcolm says, but I know he was worried. I would have been too. It'd be hopelessly optimistic not to be.

"Is he inside?" I ask. Malcolm lets go of me, looks up into my face and nods quickly.

"Come on," he says, taking my hand and dragging me inside.

I follow Malcolm into the house, the one he shares with my sister—his mother. She's asleep on the couch, resting, as she nearly always is, but I can't fix what afflicts her. It's the third occupant I'm here for.

My nephew drags me into the little dirty kitchen and sits on the floor.

"Did you manage to get the medicine?" Malcolm asks, his voice carrying that tone I hear too often: hope, tempered by the knowledge that hope isn't always enough. He's too young to sound like that.

"I got it," I tell him, taking the little ball of neural solder out of my pouch—with some difficulty, owing to my lost arm. I don't think Malcolm even notices, he's so transfixed on the tired body in front of him. "You can count on me, you know that."

He bounces side-to-side in a cross-legged position: a sort of agreement tinged with worry and impatience. "Do you think... we can keep him going like this? Just patching him up every year?" He glances back at his mother on the sofa for a moment, then down at the fuzzy heap on the floor. "I don't want to be on my own."

"You won't be," I say, taking tools out of more pouches. It's the truth. "I'll keep fixing him as long as I can. I promise."

It takes some doing, but with the three hands we've got between us—and a bit of instruction from Spyhawk, who assists with uncharacteristic focus—we manage to operate on the patched-up brain, stripping out the old, worn-out solder and replacing it with the new.

"Moment of truth," I mutter, closing everything up.

For a few long seconds, nothing happens. Then the German shepherd sniffs once, twice, opens his eyes, stands up.

"Grizzly!" Malcolm squeals, throwing his arms around the dog and burying his face in the long fur. Grizzly, for his part, lolls his tongue out and starts panting happily.

"There we go," I murmur, slumping on the floor. "All better."

Grizzly wanders over to me, Malcolm still firmly attached to his neck, and gives my face a hefty licking. "Love you too," I whisper, a tired smile creeping across my face.

"Thank you," Malcolm tells me, reaching out a hand to squeeze my shoulder. "I know it's not easy, getting the medicine for him."

"You're more than welcome," I say, meaning it.

My nephew goes back to hugging Grizzly, stroking his fur, playing with his ears, telling him what a good boy he is and how much he loves him.

"You know…" Spyhawk says quietly.

"What?"

"Just… that signal, and then it showed up… Eve, I think the Siblinghood have worked out a way to direct the Fragments."

"Oh. That's not good."

"Not really."

I can feel Spyhawk's attention split. Part of them is dwelling on pessimistic concerns about how dangerous this new development could be. The other's just watching the little boy and the big dog. "But we can think about that later," they say eventually.

I close my eyes, unwilling to hold back sleep any longer.

"You can ask now," I say quietly as I begin to drift off.

"I don't think I need to," says Spyhawk.

I fall asleep with a smile on my face.

>entry #5

>entry name:

GALLOWGATE BLUES

>

>

>entry author: JUDE REID

>

>

>access author info

>Jude lives in Glasgow and writes in the narrow gap between her work as a surgeon, raising her kids an trying to wear out a border collie. She's co-creator of th Podcast Audiodrama *Tales From The Aletheian Societ* and her short fiction has appeared in numerou anthologies and magazines. She's an active member o the Horror Writers' Association, and takes her coffee wit oat milk.

>Tweets: @squintywitch | hunterhoose.co.uk

>show entry_

It's raining in New Glasgow, but then it always is. It falls in sheets through the night, smearing neon signs into puddles of blue, pink and green on the tarmac. If you looked up, you'd see the towers and domes of the merchant city, built with the proceeds of human misery three centuries ago, and past those, the lead-grey sky, but no one ever does. Looking up means taking your eye off what's happening at ground level, and that's a mistake no one gets to make twice.

"You good?" Cordie asks me through the bead in my ear, as I back the van into the narrow lane a block north of the river.

"I'm the best and you know it."

I imagine her eyes rolling as she leans over the mic. "Yes, Kelpie, you're the best. The merch still in one piece?"

"Same number of pieces it was when I picked it up."

All things considered, it'd been a pretty neat job, even if I say so myself. Credit where it's due, though: Cordelia had put the prep in, like she always does. All I'd had to do was be in the right place at the right time with the right dose of tranquiliser, dump the driver and turn up for the collection perfectly on time.

Now I'm parked in an alley with a Tunnock & McCowan van, rocking a cherry-red-and-white uniform that makes me look like a stick of Edinburgh rock, waiting for whoever Gallowgate Biocorp, Tunnock's biggest and only real corporate rival, are going to send to pick it up. The two corporations pretty much have Glasgow stitched up between them, though the rumour is that Tunnock is working on something big—something they're calling the Godkiller, supposed to be instant death to hardware—that's going to cement their hold on the city for good. Sounds like the usual bullshit. I'll believe it when I see it.

I pop the driver's door and stretch my legs out into the alley. The rain's falling with the same soft drizzle hiss that's the soundtrack to every waking minute of my life, but there's something else coming from the back of the van. I walk round to the back doors, wondering if I'm hallucinating. I open the doors. I'm not.

It's been years since I heard it, but I know what a sleeping kid sounds like. It's the same sound my sister used to make on the other side of the mattress in the squat where we grew up, back before I got into the contracting business. Rosie had been the reason I got into the business in the first place, but by the time I'd earned enough for a decent room, food and the meds she needed, the damage was irreversible. I try not to think about Rosie these days, not if I can avoid it. On a job like this, I need to be sharp.

There are two bolts holding the crate shut. They're nothing fancy, just the kind of fastenings you'd find on an old-fashioned door, somewhere too poor for decent electronic locks. It seems like an odd choice for holding precious cargo, but I draw them back anyway, standing aside as the front drops open.

The kid's nine or ten, all spindly limbs and oversized joints. Brown skin, a few shades lighter than mine. Her scalp is covered with black stubble and punctuated with LEDS and jack-points. She's too young for that shit by anyone's measure, wearing pale grey pyjamas printed with brightly coloured unicorns. At the squeak of the crate's hinges, she opens her eyes.

"You good, Kelpie?" Cordie asks through my earpiece. I subvox a command and break the link. She'll reconnect, of course, but it'll take her a few minutes. I have a sudden need for uninterrupted thought.

"Who the hell are you?" I ask the kid.

She doesn't answer. Her eyes are wide and unfocused. She's drugged, maybe.

Here's what I should do: swing the crate door shut, drive the bolts home, go and sit in the cab like a good girl and wait for Tunnock and McCowan to show up.

Here's what I do instead. I pick the kid up and stick her in the passenger seat in the cab, slam the rear doors shut and drive, the unlocked crate rattling wildly about in the back.

"Kel! What's going on!"

Cordie again. I subvox my bead off.

"Kel, for God's sake—" This time she's on the van's

speakers. A nice trick. Cordie's good at what she does. I look around for a switch to turn her off, but it's too well hidden.

"It's a hell of a powerplay, but you keep this shit up and you're going to get us killed!"

"It's not a powerplay, Cordie." I turn the van and head for the North Bridge. I just need to get someplace quiet, where I can clear my head and work out what the hell my next move is going to be.

"Whatever you're doing, you're not thinking straight. Your vitals are starting to look a little on the stressed side…"

Maybe Cordie's right. Maybe I'm not thinking clearly. I take a deep breath, trying to slow my racing thoughts and thudding heart.

"Ditch the van and hand over the damn merchandise, Kel. We get the money and everyone goes home happy."

I risk a glance at the passenger seat, the kid staring back, her fingers digging into the seat covers. "Yeah. About the merchandise."

"What about it? If you think we're going to get a better price from someone else you're wrong; both of us'll end up at the bottom of the Clyde—"

"What the hell's in the crate, Cordie?"

The nature of the merchandise isn't something I usually need to know, but I can't believe Cordie would set me up as a kidnapper. I can hear her sigh down the speakers.

"It's a big score. Maybe the biggest out there. Remember the rumours about the Godkiller device that Tunnock were working on? The one that shuts down cyberware? Yeah. Turns out it works. Whoever owns it owns New Glasgow—and if Gallowgate can't have it, they'll settle for seeing it in the river."

"Yeah, except that's bullshit, Cordie. It's not a device in the crate, they're lying to you—"

Bullets rip through the van's door and I swerve crazily to the side. There's a bike alongside the driver's door, the helmeted rider aiming a heavyweight pistol straight at my head. On reflex, I jerk the wheel towards them. The gun fires again and the bullet goes wild, but I won't be that lucky again. In the mirror, I can see another bike coming up behind me.

"Cordie, we've got a problem!"

"You're damn right we've got a problem! Do you have any idea the shit we're in?"

Another spray of gunfire shatters the passenger window and I reach out to shove the kid's head down. "Footwell. Down." Then, to Cordie: "Get me a route away from them. There's something I need to show you, but not if I'm dead."

I hear her take a sharp breath in. For a moment she's silent. "Ok," she says at last. "There's an alley on your left. Turn. Now."

There's barely time to react. I wrench the steering wheel left, scraping the side of the van along the wall as it turns with a scream. In the mirror I see one of the bikers slam to a halt; another one swerves and almost falls as they narrowly avoid crashing into the building.

"It's helluva narrow, Cordie!"

"Don't worry about the damn paintwork! Drive!"

Pigeons explode up from the front of the van's wheels as we hurtle down the narrow alleyway. What looks at first like a trick of perspective turns out to be the alley getting significantly narrower. When we burst out the other end, we leave streaks of white paint on the stonework and a deep gouge down either side of the van. Add it to Tunnock and McCowan's list of grievances against me. The bikers burst out forty yards behind me. They're no good on corners, but give them a straight line and they'll catch up before this old banger gets up to sixth gear.

"Where am I going?"

"Straight on. Now hard left!"

I swing the van hard to its left again. The kid is staring up from the footwell, eyes wide.

I can hear Cordie typing furiously. "Stay close to the river, we'll find someplace you can ditch the van and—"

"And what?"

"And I'll think of something!"

I turn right onto the Broomilaw, ignoring the NO ENTRY sign. The van shakes as we cross the tram-tracks, but at least I don't have to dodge trams: the lines have gone unused a couple of months after their ill-judged construction. The bikes are a van's length behind me and I weave about the road as they open fire again. The van lurches sideways and I struggle to keep control, skidding almost broadside as we pass under a bridge. Rear tyre's gone, I think, or maybe both. Metal screams on tarmac and the air fills with the smell of burning rubber as I gun the engine again and we judder onto ancient cobblestones and a fresh row of bullet-holes punctuate the van.

"Stop!" the kid shrieks and I slam the brakes. An armoured limo's been parked broadside across the narrow riverside road, blocking our way. Out of the corner of my eye I see one of the bikers draw level, then they're blasted from the bike in a volley of bullets. A second later the same thing happens to the other biker, then two bodyguards and an exec in a sharp suit step out from behind the limo. It's painted in the distinctive red-and-silver Tunnock livery, matching the exec's silk scarf.

I glance over at the kid, who's starting to look more awake now, then back to the radio.

"Cordie, I think we've got a welcoming committee."

There's a long silence at the other end of the line. Then: "Kel, listen to me. I know you're good, but this merch is the literal definition of too hot to handle."

"There is no merch," I begin, but she doesn't even draw breath. "It's a kid, Cordie. Who is she?"

She ignores me. "Believe me, there's nowhere you can fence this, no one who can afford to pay what it's worth. We don't have a choice."

A rock sinks in the pit of my guts. "You've sold me out."

"Kel, I'm saving your life!" She sounds close to tears. "They're willing to offer us a bonus. A big one. Hand over the goods and you can walk."

There's no time to process any of this. Instead, I turn to the kid. "I guess they're here to pick you up. You want to go with them?"

Her dark eyes go wide. "No."

"Your parents? They work for Tunnock and McCowan?" I'm starting to wonder who the kid's related to—the CEO maybe, if they're going to go to this bother to get her back.

She glares at me from the footwell, a mouse staring out of a trap. “I’m not going.”

“That’s not up to you.”

I get out of the van, my hands held up where they can see them. The executive is leaning against her car door with a vape hanging from her lips, totally relaxed despite the rain sheeting down. The bodyguards look nasty, the SMGs in their hands even nastier.

“Looks like I’ve got something you want,” I say. The exec takes a long draw on the vape, then puffs out a cloud of lilac coloured smoke.

“I’ve got to admire your guts,” she says, her North K-side accent high and nasal. “If not your smarts. Still. Return what’s stolen and we’ll say no more about it.” She waves a languid hand towards the dead bikers. “Otherwise you can follow the example of Gallowgate’s other employees.”

I shrug, and toss the van keys to the nearer of the two goons. “Take it. It’s all yours.” I turn my back and start to walk away.

“I don’t think so, Ms Garrioch.”

So she knows my full name. I chalk up another point on Cordie’s account; I’ll be having words with her once I get out of this. If I get out of this.

“You can stay right where you are until the package is safely back in my possession. Then, and only then, you can leave.”

She’s lying, but then, so am I.

“Hey, can’t blame a girl for trying.”

I lean back against the bonnet, feigning nonchalance, as the mook goes round the back of the van.

“Mind if I vape?” I ask.

The exec waves an indifferent hand. The bodyguard, attuned to her slightest movement, flicks his eyes to the left and that’s all I need. Without conscious action, my pistols are in my hands, and I throw myself backwards across the bonnet of the van, neon lasers rasping through the air as they turn the rain to vapour. The SMG in the bodyguard’s hand stutters, but the bullets go wide. I risk a quick glance over the bonnet and snap off another shot. This time I’m rewarded with the sight of his face lit in pink as the energy beam catches him in the chest. He goes down, hard, and lies twitching in the rain.

The other guy must've worked out something's wrong by now, but any hope of him blundering round the van turns out to be in vain. The exec's nowhere to be seen, probably back in her AV while she waits for me to be gunned down in a rain of bullets. I drop and I wriggle into the narrow gap between the van and the ground. I can just make out the silhouette of a booted foot as he creeps around the van's flank. Another step and he'll be level with the passenger window; if the kid doesn't have the good sense to keep her head down then all of this has been for nothing. I shoot him in the ankle and he stumbles. I follow it up with a second, and finish him off on the ground with a third.

I'm wriggling backwards when there's an almighty shriek that fills my ears from every angle. The van's being shoved backwards with what must be superhuman strength. I'm lying on my belly in the rain, exposed on all sides, and the exec is standing in front of me. Her suit's not looking so great, but she's not even breathing heavily. I should have guessed that an exec from a cyberware company would have been fitted with a selection of their own tech.

I roll away an inch ahead of the burst of light that sears from her fingertips—implanted digiweapons, nice—and fire off a few bursts of my own. She leans back so quickly it seems that she's moving faster than the light itself, then rewards me with another spray of multicoloured light. The kid's still in the van. I risk a glance at it and see that it's spun so the passenger side is facing away from the deadly woman in the suit. I make a run for it. My fingertips are brushing the doorhandle when the taser locks into the meat of my calf. Pain arcs up through my leg into my back, my chest, my head. I try to move but nothing obeys. At least I don't feel anything when my face smacks into the cobblestones.

The exec's high-heeled shoes splash as she walks towards me, her pace unhurried. Her gloved hand, the fingertips still warm from the energy discharge, rolls me over so I can feel the rain on my face. Blood is running down my upper lip into my mouth. She bends down to put her face close to mine, so close I can smell the bubblegum sweetness from her vape.

"Goodbye, Ms Garrioch," is all she says.

I close my eyes and wait.

And nothing happens.

Terror is replaced by irritation as I open my eyes. Surely the bitch could at least get on with murdering me instead of grandstanding in the rain, but the look on her face is one of total confusion. She's staring at her fingertips like they've betrayed her, but it's only when she draws the handgun and that, too, fails to obey that she starts looking at the van. The kid's standing there, the row of LEDs sparking on her scalp, her lips moving as she subvoxes a series of commands. Smoke is rising from the exec's fingertips. She screams as her implants spark and smoke, one after another, blowing her perfectly manicured nails to hell.

"I'm not going back," the kid says.

The exec stumbles to her feet, then I hear the crack-fizz of something shorting out inside her skull. She falls forward, faint plumes of smoke rising from her ears and eyes.

The kid helps me up, or more like drags me back to the van and props me against it until my limbs decide to listen to what my brain is telling them.

"You're the device," I croak. "Doomsday. Godkiller."

She shrugs. "They made me that way. I didn't want it."

I close my eyes and listen to the rain. In the distance there's sirens, too far away to tell if they're coming for us. Five bodies on the ground, two bikes, an armoured Tunnock and McCowan limo and the crippled van. And us.

I unplug everything I can from my jack points, and drop them one after another into the water. I point to the processor that sits under the skin of my right temple, conveniently adjacent to the vox behind my ear. "Can you take care of these without frying my brain?" I ask her.

The kid looks thoughtful, nods, and then I go briefly deaf as something implodes in my right ear. When my hearing comes back I can hear Cordie shouting through the van's speakers, an unfamiliar note of panic in her voice. "Kel? I lost your vitals, can you hear me? You still there? Shit, Kel, don't be dead!" There's a *thunk* as she slams her hand into the table by the mic. I suppose I should be flattered that she's going to miss me.

She's still shouting as I release the handbrake and roll the van slowly into the Clyde. Sounds like she's crying. I'd feel a lot guiltier if she hadn't just sold me out.

The van rolls forward and slides under the water with a gurgle. There's ten feet of silt down there and a fast-flowing current to carry anything that moves out to sea. Plenty of reasons not to find a body.

"Sure you don't want to go back?" I ask the kid. She nods.

"I'm sure."

"We've got a long walk ahead of us then."

"Where are we going?"

"North," I tell her. "Out of New Glasgow."

I figure we'll find someplace with room for an ex-contractor and a kid, no questions asked. We're going to need food, a ride, somewhere to sleep, a pair of new names.

What happens after that, I've got no idea, but there's plenty of road out there. And when I look up past the neon and the sandstone towers, it turns out there's plenty of sky.

>entry #6

>entry name:

MUMBAI

>

>

>

>

>entry author: KASIA KACZMAREK

>

>

>access author info

>Originally from Poland and forged in Mumbai, Kasia is London-based filmmaker and commissione screenwriter. Published in 2019 in the *Oscurit* anthology with her debut short story "Calibrate", she' now also pushing her sci-fi fantasies onto prose reader and sizing up a full-length manuscript.

>Instagram: @kasia.jmk | circumsolar.co.uk/kasia.html

>show entry_

Theft is wrong. Ragnee knew that, of course, but there was so much wrong with Mumbai at the brink of the new century that she didn't feel bad. At least she admitted it was a crime. To herself only, so far, but it wasn't her fault she was never caught.

It also wasn't her fault that her pious parents fell for the babies born with multiple limbs and trunks for noses as harbingers of the return of the demigods. To the psalms of the pundits, they disconnected the internet, TV, even bloody electricity, and purged and purged, awaiting the mythical Adityas. If they ever left the slums, like Ragnee did to hunt for power banks now that she had no other way to charge her rescued tablet, they'd see that, south of Worli, genetic modifications were old news.

If they ever climbed the balconies of the high-rises, they would have seen that there was nothing left beside the gargantuan slum and the island of skyscrapers. No more local colonies, no more cricket grounds; only the richest, believing they are the demigods, and the poorest, desperate for that to be true. Desperate for a promise of an existence above the smog, away from the parched ocean shores.

Escalation of economic disparity and abolition of the middle class in the late 21st century was the course Ragnee was hoping to download the night she met Arjun. As every night since finding the tablet, she would choose a balcony, crack into the Wi-Fi, start downloading the next lesson and scout the flat for power banks while it progressed. Once hidden in the auto-rickshaw abandoned by the rail tracks, she would listen to the lectures and complete the interactive exercises, making sure there's enough battery left for her to download the next class and that she's home before Maa was up for the purging pooja prayer.

As every night, the residents of the flat she had chosen had already moved to one of the rooftops for a night of debauchery or got knocked out with the latest breed of benzodiazepines. Like with modern Mumbai architecture, there was no in-between.

That's why she wasn't particularly careful when searching the small bedroom of the penthouse. She even giggled out loud. The *small* bedroom could fit her entire slum dwelling inside, along with the annex for auntie Pritu and the women's communal washrooms.

"What's so funny?" asked a husky voice.

Ragnee froze. It dawned on her she had no escape strategy. She had never needed one.

"Don't worry, I can't exactly sneak up on you and hurt you."

She turned around slowly, bracing herself, but there was no one. No one was standing in her way to the balcony. She could make it in one leap—

"Your download isn't finished yet. You're safe to wait here until it's done."

"Why?" None of this made sense to Ragnee.

"Everyone else in this house is knocked out on the newest, even stronger psycholeptics. I could scream for hours for their help and it wouldn't so much as disturb their dreams, which you obviously know, too. That's why you're here. You're also here to download hands down my favourite Remote Cambridge PoliSci course. You're really smart. I'd be really not smart to kick you out of my bedroom."

Ragnee just about managed to keep the corners of her lips from lifting. She knew better than to be endeared by sexualisation, but now that it finally happened to her, it felt victorious.

"Sorry, not in a creepy way," continued the now-potential lover, and Ragnee had to accept that the certainty of his designer-genes' good looks enticed her. "Point is, we're both eloquent enough to stay away from the party drugs and the sleeping drugs. We should talk till dawn about the nature of reality."

Ragnee laughed. She decided to believe he was exactly her type of funny, rather than a helpless misfit.

"Nature of reality is such that if you expect a girl to stay in your bedroom until dawn, you need to show her your face first," she teased, and she couldn't believe she was doing it. "Not in a creepy way."

He laughed. He teased her back for descending from the intellectual planes so quickly. Before she knew it, she was stretched out on the couch, talking about never sitting on one before throughout the fifteen years of her life.

His name was Arjun, he was sixteen and studying extramurally at a top private school in the European Federation, somewhere in Switzerland.

Right around the obligatory "should we still be spending resources on space exploration if we can healthily procreate only on Earth" discussion, she spotted a little diode, blinking in the far corner in sync with the voice.

She asked about zero-gravity compatible artificial wombs and let him perorate about the need for a functioning digestive system to cleanse the excrements as she pussyfooted through the shadows.

The diode was actually a button in the corner of a screen. Ragnee's instincts were faster than the newfound eagerness to protect Arjun's perfect image in her mind and she pressed it.

The screen lit up in white, and Arjun's words started appearing on it as he spoke them:

"Oh. Well. Hi."

"What the hell?" was the easiest question to articulate out of the thousands zapping through Ragnee's mind.

Sighs showed the screen as Arjun's voice exhaled.

"Everything I told you is true," he replied at last. "For the past sixteen years I have been growing, from a clueless newborn, to a cheery toddler, to a shy teenage bookworm torn between the inexplicable urge to talk to you and the paralysing fear of disclosing that I'm not as smart as you."

Ragnee knew what was coming next and it physically weighed on her.

"I attended all the online classes at St Ursus and debated the European Viceroy on judiciary reforms. I didn't exactly... need a body for any of it."

Body. The word nearly lifted off the screen, Ragnee stared at it so intently.

"You're a computer," said Ragnee, covering her heartbreak.

"A software," replied the voice. Ragnee refused to give it a human name. "If we found you a tablet with enough memory, you could take me with you. I'd be a great rich household-ransacking companion. Could hack into security systems, access power grids and locate charging units. And clearly, could talk us out of any trouble."

Ragnee couldn't help but laugh and she hated that.

"Or..." *grunts* showed the screen, "you could come meet me..."

"What?" uttered Ragnee before she could come up with something eloquent.

"Second drawer on the left. There should be a couple of VR sets there. May be safest to take them all in case one runs out of battery. Not sure if they're charged."

Ragnee reached for the drawer and noticed the first rosy sunbeams glimmering on the handle.

"Shit. I need to go," she whispered.

"But it's a date, right?"

"What?"

"Will you... will you log in... when you have a moment, of course, and come see me? My IP is on speed dial on the sets?"

"You're asking me out on a date? You just said you were a software?"

"I'm a perfect artificial intelligence, a faithful replica, with all the flaws, with algorithms substituting hormonal influence on my behaviour as I reach the age of human puberty. Knowing the mechanics of it doesn't make me any less desperate to see you again."

Ragnee laughed. How could she say no? She had so many questions, but there was no time. She started descending the balconies before it could all catch up with her.

She usually liked the morning pooja. Not for the religious reasons. But it was a pleasant ritual, a calm entrance into the day. She could appreciate the comfort it gave to her parents.

But that morning she could not focus on the chants. There was a boy and they talked all night. And he was a computer program. What?

The VR set weighed her pocket down during the community chores. It would have been so easy for her to volunteer to fetch water and disappear into the digital ether, but she knew she had to wait. The 'three-day rule' that guided mating rituals in the early 21st century was a laughable superstition, but there was a virtue to *playing it cool* at least until the evening.

Only there was nothing cool about rehearsing witty one-liners when sweeping the communal steps and forgetting to breathe whenever it dawned on her again that the most meaningful connection she ever formed was with a line of code.

Her plan was to sneak out during the temple teachings. After the Youth Assembly, boys and girls would march into their separate chambers to be force-fed some more gender-appropriate propaganda. No one would notice one unremarkable girl missing from the crowd.

She got to the temple early to secure a strategic spot near the door. In a grey sari she blended with the background of stone walls and pillars, which must have been why the two arriving pundits didn't think to lower their voices as they entered the chamber.

And they really should've been more careful, given that one was bringing the other up to speed on the details of the next propaganda instalment and it was nasty.

The blue-skinned toddlers certainly fuelled the imagination of the simple folk, but they never survived long. The Temple was in dire need of an adult body proclaiming their teachings to keep the believers hooked, and the influence over the state intact.

Thus, the severe genetic modifications were abandoned for the Frankenstein games—sewing heads of baby elephants onto human bodies and leaving no unholy stone unturned to breathe life into them. Unsuccessfully.

At last, the solution came from an unlikely ally. In exchange for a share in the Temple's outreach, one of the richest families from Worli, the very pit of debauchery and sin, offered them a new technology: a system of interconnected nanobots that, inserted under the skin, could revive the heartbeat, reignite the flow of all bodily fluids and massage muscles into life. A boy's body was being operated on in the dungeons since the morning. The head was going to be a perfect hybrid of elephant skull and ears, human eyes and mouth, and a long trunk for the nose. The boy's torso and muscular arms were to blend seamlessly into a baby elephant's belly and legs, ending with an adult man's feet.

But really, it was all about the microchip. Synced up with the nanobots, it could replace the brain, be it human, elephant, monkey, and unify the body as a central processor to all its parts. And it could go far beyond moving the muscles and bending the limbs. Made of RNA crystals, it was the only portable device capable of holding the most sophisticated AI in the world, a software sixteen years in the making.

Youth arriving at the temple interrupted the conniving pundits, but Ragnee already heard everything she needed to hear.

She spent the entire Assembly freaking out about the fact that she's wasting the time she should use to formulate a plan on freaking out.

She was so nervous she nearly blew it, banging into an intricately embellished column when separating from the crowd. Luckily, really no one cared about the slum kids.

She snuck into a closet half full of pundit robes—cosy support for her body as her mind was about to travel elsewhere.

Ragnee had never entered virtual reality before. It took her a moment to work out the goggles and it certainly didn't help that her hands were shaking. At last, she put the device on.

At first everything was a blur, a swirl of neon colours that gradually separated into blocks, then divided into units smaller and smaller, until they formed a discrete image of a theatre stage surrounding Ragnee. She looked around in awe, suddenly experiencing a blunt hit to the back of her head, when back in reality she inadvertently banged it against the wall of the closet.

A prompt appeared in front of her—luminescent words floating in the air. She wasn't sure if they were near or far. She couldn't fully make sense of the space around her.

The prompt instructed her to build her virtual avatar, but Ragnee had no time. She accepted whatever body parts came first in the selection, and rushed through all the other set ups, to finally arrive at the address book. It only contained one contact. Arjun.

She launched for the name—but in reality, she hit her left hand hard against the closet wall. Befuddled by the pain and the neon mirage of her surroundings transforming before her eyes, she drifted away.

She came to, finding herself on a mountain top. In the distance, other peaks pierced the shroud of clouds that separated them from the rest of the world. Even from the top of Worli's highest skyscraper, Ragnee never saw so much empty space before.

"I would've warned you about the transitions if you haven't left so abruptly," a girl was standing above her. A beautiful girl, with flowing hair and curves from the Khajuraho sculptures.

Luckily, figuring out how to speak through the avatar took Ragnee long enough to allow a different part of her brain to piece things together before talking.

"Arjun? Why are you a girl?"

"Really? The brightest intellect south of Gujarat is asking me why, given the powers to take countless varied forms, I choose to explore what lies beyond an arbitrary assignment decided over a decade ago on a whim of a code writer I never met? Who never met me?"

The stream of words was too much for Ragnee, still dizzy from the new extracarnal experience. All she could do was extend a hand to be helped up. The girl responded gingerly, and Ragnee noticed that her own palm was more of a green-and-grey scaled paw with claws as long as the webbed fingers.

"Especially given the eclectic choices you've evidently made," continued the girl, prompting Ragnee to examine the rest of her body.

Muscular, dark-skinned legs clad in a leather armour from some sort of an ancient warfare video game. Bare midriff with a pierced belly button and a heavily decorated saree blouse tightly wreathing pornographically large breasts. And was it a poodle's tail with the curly fur shaved into spheres, she could see bobbing around her ankles?

Ragnee realised how glad she was not to see the face of this macabre patchwork creature—and that very thought reminded her why she took no care designing it in the first place.

"They're going to upload you into a dead body," she blurted out. She carried on, listing all the gut-wrenching details she got from the pundits. The girl listened without a word.

Somewhere around explaining the policarbon tubes, one end shoved into the trunk, the other one forced through the nostril holes of a chopped off nose and into the lungs, the girl's image jittered and glitched.

Ragnee paused. They both stood in silence, waiting.

ZAP! Another glitch jerked the girl's body in all directions at once.

"They've started the upload," she announced in Arjun's voice. "Follow me."

"What? How?"

The girl reached for Ragnee's face and in that skipped heartbeat Ragnee thought a thousand thoughts. *Is this her first kiss? Will she feel it in VR? Is she attracted to the girl? And good gods, what face is she wearing? Does Arjun like her, or does he like the virtual face? And wait, why isn't he repulsed by the Frankestein's monster's body? Does he already know he's dying and this is goodbye?*

But all the girl did was press a button on her goggles. Once again, Ragnee lost understanding of space around her.

"Just focus on breathing, it will come naturally," whispered Arjun and she realised she was looking at the inside of the closet *as well as* the girl, standing at a distance that would place her outside the wardrobe, even though its door was closed.

"I'm connected to the chip now, I can locate it, but I'll need your hands to snatch it. Come on!"

Ragnee reached out to push the closet door open and realised her hands were still reptilian paws. But she had no time to ponder on that.

She followed the girl, running down the temple corridors as if she was one of the slum kids late to the teachings. As if she wasn't the most beautiful creature Ragnee ever saw.

As Ragnee began to run too, she noticed her own crocodilian fists bobbing up and down in her peripheral vision. She looked away and caught up with the girl.

"What's your plan?"

"We burst in, you grab the chi– chi– *tshchshch*," the glitch zigzags jittered the girl around. She kept talking, but Ragnee couldn't hear a word. She followed the girl's fading image down a spiral staircase.

By the time they reached the dungeons, the girl's legs were no longer visible. A wraith, equally beautiful and haunting, she glided through the shadows, scintillating like a candle as the glitches tore at what was left of her body.

And there was less and less of it. Suddenly, Ragnee found herself all alone in the dungeons.

"Arjun?" she whispered. "Arjun!" she screamed and it reverberated through the rows of carved columns and off the musky stone walls.

Then came the silence. A silence she's never heard before in this crowded city. A silence that threatened that she will never hear another sound again.

But then she did: pained, blood-chilling screams carried down the corridor. She followed them immediately.

They were coming from behind a door. Ragnee pounded on it and tore at the door handle, but it wouldn't budge. She could hear blood splatter and bones crashing on the other side. She kept punching the door with her calloused paws, until she could no longer ignore the pain in her knuckles. She snatched the VR goggles off to see her own meagre, bloodied fingers.

Then all the screaming stopped. The door opened with a creak, revealing an elephantine figure. Truly. Above its thick-skinned pot belly and muscular shoulders sat an elephant head blended perfectly with a kind human face.

Yet Ragnee couldn't look away from the radiant blue eyes on either side of the trunk, as piercing as they were when she first started falling for them on the virtual hillside. She didn't even notice the mauled bodies all over the surgery room.

At last, Ragnee managed to start the auto-rickshaw's engine. She watched the tutorial video countless times, but the century-old, abandoned cables wouldn't cooperate.

"Where to, sir?" she grinned into the rear mirror, but all she saw in it was Arjun slumping on the back seat, staring down miserably.

"Hey, what's wrong?" she persisted.

"I just can't believe that this is how you get to see me." His trunk quivered as he spoke.

"Need I remind you what form you just saw me in?"

"But you get to come back to your real body."

"So do you." Ragnee pulled the VR goggles down from her forehead. "Breathtaking," she said to the gorgeous girl in the back of the rickshaw.

Suddenly, she remembered she never saw her own, randomly assigned, VR face. She turned again to the rear mirror—only to see two identical, beautiful faces looking back at her.

"Seriously!" she laughed. "Countless possibilities, and still… we found each other."

At last, the girl in the back seat smiled. "The psychology teacher from St Ursus would have a thing or two to say about this," whispered Arjun.

"Well, which way is Switzerland from here?"

"West?"

"That'd be that way!" Ragnee grinned, as she drove the little rickshaw towards the setting sun.

>entry #7

>entry name:

CHASSIS

>

>

>

>

>entry author: MATT DOYLE

>

>

>access author info

>Matt Doyle is an author, pop culture blogger, and indi game developer from the UK. Matt identifies as pansexua and genderfluid, and writes speculative fiction wit diverse casts and a sci-fi grounding. Matt has release the Rainbow Award-winning LGBTQ Sci-Fi/Crime Noi series, *The Cassie Tam Files.*

>Tweets: @mattdoylemedia | mattdoylemedia.com

>show entry_

"Jenn, come on," Nick pleaded. "Just let me in."

Jenn coughed through the communication panel. "Give me one good reason why I should."

"Because I need the historical touch data..."

"Yeah, yeah. But why?"

"Because..." Nick trailed off. He let his chest rise as he mimicked a deep breath. "Because I have a daughter. I have a daughter and I can't *feel* her."

There was a moment of silence, then a quiet series of beeps rang out on the other side of the door. It slid open with a tired, well-worn *whoosh*.

"You never wanted kids," Jenn stated.

Nick studied her. She looked as weary as the door sounded, all dark rings around her eyes and a heaviness in her shoulders. It made him a little sad. "Please, Jenn. I need this."

Jenn looked at Nick up and down, but came to a stop on his face. "Your eyes haven't changed. Even against the metal, they look the same."

"The med techs spent a lot of time getting the eyes *right*. They're one of the first things we notice about someone, and often the thing we remember the clearest. So, can I come in? Please?"

She frowned, then sighed. "Fine. But no touching. First, we talk."

"Thank you." Nick replied and followed her inside. Looking around his old home, he could see that she had barely changed anything since he had moved out. Projected wall colours, sure, but the furniture was just as he'd left it.

Clearly noticing what he was looking at, Jenn said, "I picked the furniture, so it's not like it reminded me of you. Not after a while, anyway. How's... Ted?"

Nick tilted his head. "He's good."

Jenn nodded and immediately started coughing again, this time dropping onto the couch with a grunt.

"Are you..." Nick began, but Jenn held a hand up to stop him.

"It's the flu. Nothing serious, it just lingers. It's worse at night." She groaned. "So this is the new Life Chassis, huh? Silver suits you, somehow."

The flexible metal that formed Nick's face pulled back and lifted his lips into a smile. "Surprisingly easy to clean too. The Units have this, like, polishing system built in."

"The Units sound lonely to me. You can't physically visit anyone, can you? Or nobody else like you, I mean. What happens when us mere mortals die out?"

"Still morbid, I see. It's not so bad though. We do all our work remotely, using the new virtual network. We can walk, talk and do whatever else we'd do face to face that way."

Jenn grabbed a steaming mug from the little table next to her. She swallowed a mouthful, then wrapped her hands around the ceramic. "That's not the same though, is it? Or not the same as what *we're* doing. The actual contact."

"It's not that different." Nick shrugged. "Everything we could do here, we can do there. Remember, these bodies retain our original brains and all our sensory data is stored in there. If I'm walking in the virtual Central Park, I get the same scents. If someone whispers in my ear, I hear it and get the sensation of their breath. If I stroke a dog, I feel its fur." Nick's head dropped and he stared at his feet. "Or I used to."

"How does that work?" Jenn asked. "I mean, I get what you're saying about your brain, but your body is metal. Metal can't feel. It never has."

Nick held his arm out towards her. "Here. Run your hand over my arm."

Jenn blinked, considering what to do. There was definite curiosity in her eyes though and, eventually, she put the mug back on the table and placed her hand on his forearm. Her eyebrows shot up immediately and she trailed her hand up and down, even sliding between his fingers. "It's soft. And warm."

"Yes," Nick nodded. "The bodies get coated in a thin, semi-solid gel layer to simulate skin. It's technically translucent by default, but you can set your colour as you wish. Hence my silver. Though they do recommend a flesh tone when we visit '*mere mortals*' as you put it. Sorry, would you prefer that? I can change it any time."

"No, it's fine. Continue."

"The gel is filled with nanobots. They're small and high-tech, but simple in function. Basically, the waking brain knows it's not in a flesh-and-blood body. The bits that deal with physical sensations though? They still expect the same cues to come through. The nanos hold data on what sort of signals to send to the brain to complete the circuit and make it register things like touch. Both in the real and virtual world. They're like teeny-tiny, amoeba shaped apps."

Jenn glanced up at his face. "They don't mention that in the adverts."

"No, I think they worry it would reduce curiosity in the process. It all seems very alien, doesn't it?"

"It does. So, can you feel what I'm doing?" she asked, squeezing his wrist.

"No."

"How come?"

Nick gently pulled his arm away and sat back into the chair. "Both Ted and I went through the process. We knew that it was unadvisable to meet another Chassis user in real life, but… I guess we both wanted to talk about things face-to-face. Like, there's still an urge for that there, you know? Hence why the medical teams recommend maintaining relationships with non-Chassis users. So, we met up, and hugged. And *pop*."

"*Pop*?"

"Yeah. My nanos and his nanos collided. Basically, the gel layers rubbed against each other, he got some of mine, I got some of his, and the machines got confused. They overheated and went *pop*. It wasn't a problem for Ted; he just replaced the gel layer and everything was fine. I wasn't so lucky though. The touch data on mine was too heavily corrupted when it happened and when I tried to replace the gel layer, the new nanos couldn't recover it. So, I can function, but I can't physically feel when I'm touching something or being touched in either setting. Which sucks."

"And is the reason you're here." Jenn crossed her arms and narrowed her eyes. "If you're told to maintain relationships outside the process, why didn't you stop by before now? It's been two years, Nick."

"I know, but… we didn't exactly part on good terms. You were angry with me."

"Understandably."

"Yeah. And I knew that it was…" Nick let out a synthesized sigh. "I didn't want to hurt you more than I already had."

Jenn sat in silence for a moment, her pose unchanging as she stared at him. Her nose twitched. "Okay. Okay, I get it. You can take what you need. Do you mind if we keep talking though? I'll be honest with you, Nick: I know there's no going back, but I've missed this."

"Thank you," Nick replied, relief creeping into his voice. "And of course. I've missed this too."

Nick rose to his feet and took out a phone and a data cable from his hip pouch. He walked to the control panel of the main wall, hooked them up and started scrolling through to find historical data. "I'm searching for touch screen impressions that match my old physical signatures," he explained. "Everything from finger pressure to micro-movements that indicate a reaction to different sensations. The med team should be able to rebuild enough of a model to retool the nanos that way."

"Didn't they keep it on file when you went through all *that*?" Jenn asked, waving her hand at him.

"I asked that too. Do you know what they told me?"

Jenn shook her head.

"There's so much data required to get a person's full picture that they can only use it once, check if it works and then wipe the copy. The nanos store it in small chunks and transfer the data to the new set when you replace the gel. The most important point though, and the one they took the most pleasure in telling me, was this: if I didn't realize how complex the human body's responses to even simple things are, then I must be an idiot."

"Then I guess we're both idiots," Jenn laughed. "I take it there's no more physical meetings for you and Ted then?"

Nick shook his head and moved to the kitchen, hooking up to the control panel by the worktop.

Jenn followed and rested her shoulder against the doorframe. “Do you miss it? Seeing him outside the virtual environment, I mean?”

“Not really. I *did*, but seeing what happens as a result was a kick to feel better about not doing it. Plus, the virtual world for people like me is different than it is for you. Do you spend much time there?”

“A little. It's not as relaxing for me as it is for a few others in this block though.”

“It might be, if you were like me. See, the nanos really come into their own there. They link with the simulation wirelessly and make sure it feels *exactly* the same as it did when I had a flesh body.”

“But it's *not* the same, is it? It's simulated.”

“It depends how you look at it. The human body is like a big computer anyway and the way you experience things is all controlled by the brain. *It* interprets emotions, smells, tactile sensations, all by working together with the rest of the body. My brain is still human, but it works in tandem with a metal compound rather than flesh and organs. It's a different tool but yields the same results.”

“Interesting… so how long has it been since you could *feel* things?”

“Six months.”

Jenn blinked. “That's a long time.”

“Yes. It is. Do you mind if I, uhm?” Nick asked, nodding towards a door opposite the kitchen entrance.

“The bedroom? Sure. Nothing in there you haven't seen before.”

Nick smiled awkwardly and made his way to where he used to sleep. Once inside the room, he paused, looking around and remembering his time there.

“Do you miss it?” Jenn asked. “Sleep, I mean. You're on constant contactless charge, aren't you?”

“I am. It's one of the perks of the body really. I never miss a new upload on the streaming services, I'm never late for work and I get the news as it happens rather than the next morning."

"Don't you miss dreaming though?"

"I mostly had nightmares, if you remember. If I do want to dream, I can simulate it easy enough, but I haven't yet."

Jenn sat down on the bed and coughed again. "What about death?"

Nick paused and frowned at her. "I'm sorry?"

"What about death? Do you miss knowing that, one day, all of this will be over?"

"No, of course not. The idea of dying terrified me. The only reason I risked it to have *this* done was because it was a way to avoid it permanently if it worked."

"That's why I couldn't ever have it done, I think," Jenn said leaning back onto her hands. "For me, life always seemed like it should be finite. Knowing there was an inevitable end made life worthwhile. And special."

"So you're saying I'm not truly alive?"

"Honestly? I don't know. I mean, if human sensations can be reduced to data and copied into an artificial equivalent, that's one thing. But who's to say that the same applies to your general existence? Are your memories real, is it still you, or are you just a copy that doesn't know that's what it is? It's a weird thing to consider."

"Hmm... Think of it this way. There are animals out there that clone themselves. Komodo dragons, some hammerhead sharks and even sea sponges can do it. Now, those clones have the same DNA but *not* the same memories. They're new life, but identical to the parent in every way other than experience. They *are* copies, though, and you would absolutely view them as alive, right?"

"Well, yeah, because they're entirely biological. Are you saying that the Nick I knew is dead and you're like his clone child, is that it?"

"Not at all. I'm saying that Life Chassis transfers are more complete. I'm more *Nick* than Komodo Dragon Offspring A is Komodo Dragon Parent A. The only difference is the body. That surely constitutes life?"

"Like I said, I don't know. It's *different*, for sure."

"Okay, well how about this. The wallpaper in this room is projected through a touch-compatible screen. You can even set it to have butterflies and other wildlife fluttering across and reacting to your fingers. Does that make it less valid than when we had to pull out paste and have physical paper you *couldn't* interact with? Meat is printed using synthesized ingredient compounds. Does that make it less valid than when we slaughtered cows?"

"No, in both cases. Because they offer sustainable improvements."

"This is the same. No more death. No more hunger or thirst. No more need to sleep. Limited outside interaction—that will itself disappear once Life Chassis users are the only ones left—means less environmental damage. And no more physical births, meaning no more ballooning populations."

"Life but improved, huh?" Jenn sighed. "So. You and Ted have a kid. From what you just said, I'm guessing she's in the virtual world?"

"Born and will be raised. Please tell me you're not going to say that means she isn't real?"

"Of course not. I mean, I had a virtual pet once."

Nick turned to her and raised an eyebrow. "Really?"

Jenn smiled. "I'm joking, I'm joking. It's... how can I say this? The concept is beyond me philosophically, I think. Maybe I'm just too stuck on this idea that death is needed for life to exist."

Nick nodded and returned to what he was doing. "If it helps, death is technically still possible. For me, the contactless charge system failing or being physically destroyed would have the same effect, eventually. And our daughter... if all the servers were damaged, she would..." He shook his head.

"How does it work having a child virtually like that? Not judging; I'm genuinely curious."

"It's built in that we would, well, you know. As part of the process. The *act* produces a bunch of randomized virtual components that meet and are joined randomly until there's enough there to simulate an embryo. It grows for six weeks and then is born into the virtual world. From there, the child grows at a natural rate until they're an adult, then the aging stops."

"So you guys have to find virtual childminders and stuff when you work?"

"Yes. Because some experiences should be universal to create bonds. She's one year old, by the way. We called her Luna."

"You haven't been able to feel her for the entire six months? That's… Wow. I'm sorry."

Nick removed the cable from the control panel and put his phone back in his pouch. "This will help. I won't have the full sensation back, but enough to have the familiarity. Over time, they might be able to fix the rest through simulations based on new data, but who knows? Thank you though."

Jenn nodded and looked away, one arm coming up to grip the other. She rubbed her elbow absently. "Look, I should apologize. What happened to us was… I said some things I shouldn't have. Things I didn't mean. I don't hate gay people. I never have. I just wish you'd figured out who you are before I got so attached."

Nick smiled. "I'm sorry too. I really was happy being with you, just not as lovers. I could—*should*—have said something sooner."

"Yes. You should have." Jenn sighed. "But, hey. We're talking now. And I really did miss this. Look, I know it's a finite existence compared to what *you* have now, but I'd love to reconnect properly. As friends. I'd like to get to know Ted too. And maybe meet Luna one day?"

"I'd like that too. I'll talk to Ted. He was… pretty angry with you. And boy does he hold a grudge. I'm sure I can work my magic though. Even if he won't talk to you himself, there's nothing to stop *us* meeting up to chat."

"Good. I'm glad you're happy, Nick."

"And I'm glad you're… unwell and living with the knowledge that death gives your life meaning?"

Jenn laughed. "Smooth talker. Go on. Go get yourself fixed and hug your daughter."

Nick stepped out of the chamber and let the automated cooling system dry his new coating. He simulated holding his breath and touched his own arm. The familiar texture of the gel tickled his fingers and palm and his senses responded to the softness. "It really isn't the same as it was, but it's there," Nick gasped. "I can feel again."

Nick rushed to his chair and immediately logged into his shared home space. There, his husband, Ted, sat playing with their daughter. When she saw Nick arrive, Luna smiled and said, "Dar-dar."

Ted followed his daughter's gaze and his eyes lit up with a mix of hope and concern. He walked over to Nick and asked, "Did it work?"

Nick nodded. "I think so. In the Unit, definitely."

Ted picked Luna up and smiled. "Good. Someone has been dying for hug." He gave their daughter a gentle tap on the nose and held her out towards Nick.

Nick hesitated, his fists clenching instinctively as thoughts rushed through his brain. *What if it doesn't work here? What if the nanobots didn't recover enough data for anything other than physical touch?*

He closed his eyes and centred himself, relaxing and holding out his arms. The moment he felt Luna's little body against his, a smile rose to his lips. Nick's mind told him he was crying, though he knew that he wasn't. "I can feel her," he sobbed. "You hear that Luna? Daddy can feel you again."

"Yay," the child cheered, cuddling into his chest.

Nick laughed and glanced at Ted. "Jenn was fine. Unwell, but fine. She apologized for, well, everything. She wants to reconnect. And to get to know *you* better."

"Please tell me you said no," Ted replied with a grunt.

"We'll talk about it later. Right now, I'm just enjoying *this*," Nick said and squeezed his daughter tight, enjoying the warmth of her body for the first time in six months.

>entry #8

>entry name:

A HERALD IN ATHENS

>

>

>entry author: GARY MOLONEY

>

>

>access author info

>Gary Moloney is a lawyer by day and writer by nigh
from Cork, Ireland, known mainly for his work in comic
His short stories and comics have featured in a numbe
of anthologies. His debut comic, *Mixtape*, was name
Best Irish Anthology by ICN in 2018. When not locked t
his desk, he enjoys windsurfing and arguing with Cha
his aging King Charles Spaniel.

>Tweets: @m_gearoid | gumroad.com/garymoloney

>show entry_

Hermes landed in the city shortly before 6pm, just as the lights were coming on. It was different, had been for a long time. He took a deep breath and coughed out the night's air. Athens had a familiar taste, albeit with more metallic hues than he remembered. He lit a match off his winged heel and with it his cigarette. Much better. At least some things stayed the same.

The people around him had begun to stare. It was an empty stare, as if they didn't recognise him. Hermes let out a sigh, exhaling a mouthful of smoke. Of course they didn't. They started to gather as the Nodes in their heads blinked rapidly. Each searched the Hive Network of newsfeeds, live-streams and databases, curious about the man who had come from the sky. That was his cue to leave. He fixed his suit jacket, securing his satchel in the process. The streets may have been filled with neon these days, but Hermes knew where he was going. When it came to his job, he always did.

Athens had been, at least in his opinion, one of the first great city-states. It was fitting in a way that it had become one of the first great mega-cities during the era of metropolitan expansion. The entirety of what had once been Attica now stood united under one urbanised structure, a sea of concrete and metal. And still, somehow, that little shit had managed to set himself up in the dingiest part of town. The bar itself was located at the end of a dark alleyway, the kind you normally walked out of minus a wallet and a pint of blood. Hermes stood outside as its sign flashed the word "DEUS" in bright pink before fading away. Whatever else could be said about the kid, at least he had a sense of humour.

Reaching into his satchel, Hermes took out the letter and examined it. No addressee. No stamp. Just a wax seal with a lightning bolt emblem embossed on it. They still called him a 'herald', as if the gods went anywhere anymore. The Olympians didn't have much need for a herald nowadays, but a messenger? Those were always in demand. Now all he needed to worry about was not getting shot in the process.

DEUS was one of those dives built on the site of an old brewery, as if to suggest you were drinking straight from the source. Bullshit. Everyone knew they brewed off-site, but the idea was enough for some. Ideas were what DEUS served.

The patrons turned as the metallic door creaked open announcing that Hermes, the emissary of the gods, had arrived. They were not what he had expected. First, they weren't as rough-looking or as miserable as he might have thought; a mix of creative and business types, with the odd representative of the city's more traditional criminal element spread throughout. Second, their Nodes showed no sign of network activity. They neither blinked nor flashed nor lit up. And that was something that wasn't meant to be possible. In fact, as far as the herald could see, there wasn't any technology in the joint at all.

As Hermes approached the bar, he noticed one or two of the more enterprising patrons watching him carefully. They stood up, hands reaching inside jacket pockets and lingering there. Wanting desperately to share their secret with the world. The kind that hold six chambers filled with lead. The messenger snapped his fingers and the staff appeared, two serpents entwined with a set of wings adorning the top. Hermes could feel the patrons' sights on him; their hands revealed as metal clicked and fingers itched. He held the staff before him, his grip tightened, presenting it to the bartender.

"You know what this is."

The man behind the bar looked Hermes up and down. He glanced at the staff, then back at Hermes. Letting out a sigh, he made a gesture with his hand. The patrons returned to their drinks, their secrets secret once more.

Hermes sat on a stool, placing his symbol of office on the counter. A glass of wine appeared in front of him. The messenger looked at his younger brother and nodded.

"Dionysus."

"Hermes. What can I do for you?"

Much like the world, Hermes thought the God of Wine was quite different from when he last saw him. Dionysus had always been a precocious one, but the hipster-bun and the extreme v-neck were certainly new. They each took a sip of their drinks; say what you want about his brother, but he knew how to treat himself. At least some things stayed the same.

The demi-god had never really gotten over the Decree of Non-Interference, leading to a millennia long protest which saw him rarely interact with his fellow Olympians. Hermes was lucky if he saw Dionysus once every few centuries. It was a move their father described as 'typical', though Hermes would have called it 'expected'. Thinking of their father, the messenger slid the letter across the bar.

"Got a delivery for you."

"I can see that."

"Think you should open it."

"Suppose I don't."

"Probably not a clever idea."

"Let's say I'm not a clever man."

"Well, if I recall correctly, he's pretty handy with those lightning bolts of his."

"As if he would..."

"It's right there on his seal."

"He'd hardly hold a grudge against me."

"S'funny, I remember Sisyphus saying something similar."

Thinking about it for a minute, Dionysus sucked in the air through his teeth.

"Fair point," he said.

Dionysus fiddled with the envelope, tapping it against his hand before laying it flat on the counter and sliding it back to the messenger. Unopened. The God of Wine poured himself another glass, filling the messenger's too. Hermes downed his in one go.

"What the fuck are you doing here, D?" he asked. "You must have known the Big Man would send someone to bring you home."

Dionysus traced the rim of his glass with his index finger attentively.

"Did you feel it when you first arrived?" he said, still transfixed by the motion.

"Feel what?"

"The anonymity."

"I don't..."

"They've forgotten us, Herms."

"Listen, D..."

"After everything we did for them!"

"Because it's... it's not our world anymore!"

"And maybe that's the problem!"

The two brothers said nothing for a moment. Arguing was what their kind did best, it was how they passed the time. Without proxies, however, the stakes were much higher than before and there were so few of them left. So they stuck to words instead. Dionysus filled their glasses as he did the silence.

"It's not just us, you know. They forget everything unless it goes through their network: friends, birthdays, the news... you name it. Even then nothing stays with them very long." He pointed at Hermes. "I mean, you literally flew into the city a few hours ago and it's barely on their radar."

"D, I get it, but you really need to understand this: they're no longer our concern."

"You sound just like him. A bit rich of him to swan in and say there was to be 'no more meddling' after all he'd done."

"He had his reasons."

"Now you sound more like Athena."

Hermes let out a sharp laugh; they both did. He couldn't help it: the kid always did have a sense of humour, even back in the old days. The invention of hangovers had been a particular favourite. Not that it mattered. The Big Man had made his decision and it was up to Hermes to enforce it. Still, there was the small matter of the patrons and their Nodes.

"What's the deal with the mortals? They're all... disconnected."

"So you noticed." Dionysus said, in a tone that seemed overly pleased about being asked. "Follow me".

Descending into what had been the old brewery, Hermes' nostrils filled with the whiff of fresh hops. They came to an area with two large copper pots connected to other contraptions and what appeared to be an active fermentation tank. Off to the side were stacks of crates: each filled with hundreds of beer bottles. Picking one up for closer inspection,

Hermes could see each had the words “Boon of Bacchus” emblazoned on brightly coloured labels in bubbly font.

“Craft beer… Are you serious, D?”

“It wouldn’t have been my first choice, but if there’s one thing these ‘Neo-Philistines’ love more than staying online it’s micro-brews.”

“Olympus holds some of the finest wines on any plane of existence, many of which you’ve had a hand in making, and you would defy the Decry for the sake of hipster lager?”

“Technically it’s an ale, but yes, I would.”

“What is so damn special about this drink that you would risk the wrath of Zeus for it?”

“Because it allows them to hear me again!”

Grabbing the Boon from his older brother’s hand, Dionysus sat on a crate and popped the cap off with his thumb. He wrung his fingers through his hair as he took a drink from the bottle. The demi-god allowed the ale to linger in his mouth before swallowing. Staring at the bottle, his words became soft and strained.

“Here’s the thing, Herms. The wine was only ever part of the gig. Madness. Ecstasy. Fertility. They’re all anyone seems to remember. Nobody talks about the art.”

“Because it wasn’t your job!”

“I don’t have to be the god of something to be a fan. The world was quieter then, it allowed them to hear inspiration as it whispered to them. It wasn’t always my voice but on occasion, when they treated themselves to fruit of the vine, I’d suggest a note or lyric. Just enough to get the ball rolling.”

“This… this is exactly why we aren’t allowed in the mortal realm…”

“They may have worshiped me, but I worshiped them too! I worshipped their potential; their ability to create something from nothing. Don’t you think they deserve another chance at making it work?”

Tears began to drip down Dionysus’ face, he wiped them away and tapped his head where the Node might have been if circumstances had been different.

“There’s so much information flowing in and out every second of every minute of every hour of every day. It’s a wonder they even function. Most are lucky if they're able to keep themselves together. Some aren't. That's where my Boon comes in."

Clutching a fresh bottle of ale, Dionysus gestured towards the copper pots.

"The Boon doesn't quieten their mind totally, just the part of it that's wired up, temporarily severing their connection to the Hive Network. It gives them a moment's respite. Just the slightest bit of time to be by themselves. And, hopefully, time to be inspired."

Gusts of air came rushing towards Dionysus as Hermes crossed the room to grab his brother. The messenger gritted his teeth, looking into his brother's eyes. How could he be so foolish? No more meddling: that was the rule. No exceptions. Too much potential for abuse. There was a logic to it or, at least, there had been.

"The Big Man expects you back in Olympus within a fortnight," he said, taking the bottle from Dionysus. "I can't just leave you here to your own devices. Not now."

"You'll have to drag me there," Dionysus said through laboured breaths. "This is my home, Herms. It always has been."

Hermes sighed, letting Dionysus go. The world around him may have changed, but his brother hadn't.

"We thought all that stuff was just part of your "rebellious" phase," the messenger said, opening the bottle of Boon. "Kinda hoped you'd get over it after a few millennia."

"Blame my mother."

"Don't worry, we do," Hermes said, before taking a sip of the ale. It was good. Almost as good as the wine. Almost. He sat down on the floor, leaning up against the closest copper pot. Dionysus joined him.

"Come on, Herms. You saw the bar. You can't tell me you don't miss this place? We had some good times in Athens over the centuries."

"Look, I'm not saying I wouldn't like to visit every now and again."

He passed the bottle to Dionysus.

"There are only so many tricks you can pull on the same immortal before it gets old. But that's the thing, D. I enjoyed messing with them. You? You just enjoyed being with them."

Dionysus picked at the label on the bottle.

"I used to. I'd like to again. With a bit of help, maybe I could."

Hermes remembered Athens as it once was. He remembered how quiet it could be. A luxury it seemed in a place that still bore the name, but not the soul.

"Your little operation. It's... impressive, to say the least," the messenger said gesturing at the various brewing apparatus that surrounded them. "You built all of this yourself?"

The God of Wine shrugged, spilling some of the ale.

"I have a few people helping out, you met them earlier, but it's mostly just me."

Hermes nodded, taking the bottle from his brother and with it a long swig.

"I like that. Very enterprising of you. From what I've seen it's rare to find small business ventures in this world anymore. Seems to me like something to be encouraged."

Confused, the God of Wine narrowed his eyes. A slight smile appearing on his face.

"What are you saying, Herms?"

"I'm saying... wine has always greased the wheel of commerce. Sounds like there's opportunity for mischief there. And I'm a god with quite a lot of time on his hands."

The messenger took his cigarettes from his pocket and lit one, tossing the rest to Dionysus.

"If I learned anything from our father, sometimes it takes the youngest of us to shake up to the old order. So, what would you say to my not reporting back to the Big Man just yet?"

"I'd say that's mercurial thinking on your part."

The two gods stood up. Each looking the other in the eyes.

"I'd say you were starting to sound like your old self."

"Good. Because if we do this I'm going to need a job and from my understanding of this whole 'email' thing, I doubt you'll need a messenger."

Hermes placed his hand on his brother's shoulder. Dionysus did the same.

"A messenger? No. But a herald? That's something I can work with."

>entry #9

>entry name:

ONLY HUMAN

>

>

>

>

>entry author: EMMA O'CONNELL

>

>

>access author info

>Emma O'Connell is a fantasy lover. She spends her fre
time creating worlds in her head and occasionall
making attempts to nail them down to words. The focuse
of her writing tend to be relationships, motherhood, lov
grief, and mental health – real-world topics in fantas
settings. She is also an editor, specialising in fictio
with five years of experience.

>Tweets: @emmas_edit | emmasedit.com

>show entry_

The surgeon looks at me with sympathy in his eyes.

"How did you end up here, David?"

Text hovers over his face, superimposed on my vision. His name, although he's introduced himself already to be polite, is Doctor Ahmad Sadiq. He's forty-seven years old. He likes classical music and riding his bike on the weekends. He's also considered a texpert in chips, according to the first line of his Wikipedia entry.

He's not speaking English, but the translation tech is so flawless that it almost sounds like he is. I wouldn't be able to tell if I didn't have a tiny transcript of his words running along the bottom of my vision, both in Arabic and English.

I bite down on my bottom lip, trying to control my panic. An alert goes off when I break the skin, flashing up before I even feel the pain and taste the blood. I'm trying desperately not to dwell on what's about to happen to me, but a single thought is all it takes to have thousands of search results explode into my mind: articles and videos and podcasts about what the surgery looks like, how the process works, the campaigns against it because it turns people into 'subhumans', speculations on what it feels like *afterwards*.

"I made a mistake," I tell Dr Sadiq. It sounds cliché, but it's true. I never meant for it to go this far.

I guess everyone says that, though.

I didn't kill anyone, or anything like that. It started out as a game, more than anything, just to see how many numbers we could fiddle without the system alert going off. A challenge between me and my friends. It was fun. It wasn't until they arrested me that I really thought of how those numbers meant something to someone else. I never asked whose bank account it was. I guess I don't really want to know.

He doesn't press me for more. He can probably see some details on it through his own chip, anyway—I don't know how much is pub-dom knowledge. I could find out, but it seems like a waste of my last few minutes as a real person.

"This won't hurt," he says instead, his voice gentle and professional. "The anaesthetic is completely painless and when you wake, you will only have a small scar at the site of removal."

I nod. My brain is spinning, frantically trying to hold on to something that will give me some comfort, some reassurance. My heart monitor starts going insane and the recommendation to *Take a Deep Breath* flashes up in red. I keep trying to focus on saying a proper goodbye to this, to all of it, but the memories I so badly want to keep are somehow eluding my grasp.

"Do you have any other questions?" the surgeon asks, checking the apparatus again and holding the mask in front of my face. Some diagrams pop up telling me how the anaesthetic works, and his words trigger a list of some of the most frequently asked questions by patients at this stage. None of them seem worth asking to me, and 'How do I avoid this?' isn't one of them. I shake my head.

"Okay," he says, and the mask comes down over my nose and mouth. "Relax and take a deep breath for me."

The alert flashes again, this time telling me how my system is responding to the anaesthetic. I get about three seconds of watching its progress through my body before I black out.

Afterwards, just before I leave the clinic, they tell me that the adjustment period is normal. Apparently no one can function without their chip in the first two weeks. It's like you regress right back to childhood, or maybe even before. You have to re-learn so much stuff that your brain just can't cope with it. Your body goes into overload and basically shuts down.

That describes it pretty well. I only remember flashes of those two weeks. I remember retching violently into a toilet. I remember faces blurring as I tried to match them to a non-existent database. I remember not eating enough because I didn't have my calorie count or nutrition plan anymore and being surprised when my clothes started to get loose. I remember the sheer agony of that incessant, blinding *silence*—that screaming void where there used to be colour and sound and information and people.

That one hasn't got much better.

The others have, though. I was honestly surprised when I started to figure out how much I should eat based on how full I felt, or going for a pee when I needed it instead of when my bladder monitor went off. Those were small victories, but they got lost quickly in the frustration of it all. I felt so *slow*, so clumsy, so utterly blind and helpless. I was struggling to sleep, too, because I couldn't play my insomnia playlist at night like I used to. I had all the time in the world to lie there and think about what I've become.

The cybernet is full of people making fun of guys like me. They call us no-teks—which is an idiotic name if you ask me. There's a subreddit dedicated to us and everything. I don't know if it's better or worse that I used to be one of those people, laughing at the losers who fucked up so badly their basic human rights had to be revoked. Maybe it's a good thing I'll never be able to access those forums again.

Now that I've remastered some basic functions, I've been signed out of the clinic and assigned to one of the no-tek community centres. I have no idea what to expect, and my heart monitor should be screaming at me about my increasing panic as I walk into the office, only of course it doesn't.

The man waiting for me is nondescript and smooth and grey. He has a smooth grey voice and cool grey eyes and I feel like I can't trust him, but I have no idea whether that feeling is founded or not, because I can't see *anything* about him. All I know is his name, because he's wearing a badge with it on.

"Welcome to Refuge, David. We're very happy to have you here."

I clench my jaw and don't reply.

"We believe strongly in positive rehabilitation, David. Whether your sentence will allow your chip to be reinserted or not, here at Refuge we want to emphasise that it's possible to live a fulfilling and happy life with no augs or biotech."

He sounds like a fucking robot. He probably is. The staff here are allowed chips, of course. Do they actually believe this bullshit they spout?

When I was younger I never really got why becoming a no-tek was such a big deal. The no-tek coms are supposedly more like rehab than prison; after a few months you can receive visitors, and many no-teks are allowed to go home, too, even if they're monitored closely—depending on the terms of their sentence. As a kid the idea of being locked in one room seemed worse than anything else they could do to me.

It's almost funny how stupid I was.

The grey man seems to be waiting for me to reply and when I stay silent, his eyes tighten slightly before he goes on. "To that end, we have a mentor system. You'll be assigned a mentor from among our residents—someone who has been here longer than five years. They'll help you adjust and continue to adapt to life without your chip."

I don't say anything. What is there to say? *I'm* the robot here now, not him. I'm nothing more than skin and bones.

When I'm introduced to Michael, I want to laugh at first. He's so… ordinary. He looks kind of like my dad, if he was a bit stouter and wore glasses. (*Glasses*. What is this, the middle ages?) Michael has a round, friendly face and eyes that seem to smile all the time. The only unusual thing about him is that he's missing a hand, but that's pretty normal around here. Loads of no-teks have scars or missing limbs where biotech used to be. They're—*we're*—allowed prosthetics, but only with basic functionality. No tech. Michael's left hand is an ugly, old-fashioned mixture of shiny plastic and metal.

Because he looks so cheerful, it takes me by surprise when he sits me down in our room on my first evening and starts talking about ground rules.

"This will be difficult, and if you want to survive, you'll need to listen to me," he warns me, and for a second I get a glimpse of a totally different man beneath the friendly exterior—someone who's seen hardship, someone who won't bend easily to others. I actually get a momentary chill of fear.

Then his face creases in a smile and he looks like a fat, balding monk again.

"This is an opportunity, David," he says. "You've been handed a gift. I want to help you make the most of your freedom."

I try to hide the disbelief on my face, but he picks up on it surprisingly quickly, considering that he doesn't have a chip analysing my expressions.

"You don't agree?" he asks, still smiling.

I feel guilty being rude to him—it feels kind of like swearing at a teacher—but the words come out anyway. "This is a punishment," I point out flatly. "It's the literal opposite of freedom." Everyone gets chipped, for God's sake, no matter which country or community you're from. Other augs depend on economic status, so not everyone has the same ones, but the chips are universal. Having it taken away... it's like a reversal of everything we consider human nature to be.

Michael shakes his head. I wish there wasn't so much kindness in those eyes. It makes me feel bad for how delusional he clearly is.

"I've been here twenty years," he says, "and I know better. This is what we're supposed to be, David. *This* is humanity; freedom from the technology that ensnares and controls us." He waves the prosthetic hand, as if we're in a palace rather than a room that resembles student accommodation. "I'm going to help you rediscover what it means to be human."

I pretend to throw up when he's not looking.

Michael's 'rehabilitation' project is frustratingly simple and just as boring as him. Firstly, I have to go outside every morning and take a deep breath. Secondly, I have to sprout a plant from seed. Thirdly, I have to learn how to bake bread.

"What do you see?" Michael asks me on the third day while we're doing our deep breaths, me feeling like a total twat. I look at him like he's an idiot.

"Nothing," I snap. There's *nothing* here. Nothing in my head but my own fucking voice.

He puts his real hand on my arm for a second, but doesn't say anything. The sympathy in his eyes makes me want to punch him.

To avoid getting the same response again, I try a different tack on day five. "I see trees," I tell him with fake astonishment, but my plan immediately backfires when his face lights up as if I've just given him the greatest present ever.

"Good! Good! What else?"

Feeling slightly guilty, which is stupid, I make a show of looking around. Actually, the com centre is in a pretty decent place. It has these huge grounds that we're allowed to walk around whenever we want, and they're full of trees and flowers. Of course, I don't know anything about them because I don't know their names, their properties, their history—anything. I'm reduced to just what I can see and smell and touch. Like an animal.

"Purple flowers," I say to Michael, pointing at a bed of them nearby. He grins and nods and tells me that I'm doing great. I roll my eyes as soon as he looks away.

When I look back at the flowers, though, I realise that I picked them out because they remind me of the colour of my sister's curtains when we were kids. Pretty.

The stupid plant drives me up the wall. For some reason I thought it would be easy. Stick the seed in the soil, water it daily, right? And then a plant comes up. But nothing happens for *ages*. Eventually it turns out first that I watered it too often, and then not often enough. I take a surprising amount of pleasure in throwing plant #2 out of our window and watching the pot smash against the path outside. Michael just calmly puts plant #3 in its place. I glare at it and make up my mind that this time I'll get it right, come hell or high water. I am not about to be defeated by a chilli plant.

When the tiny green sprout starts to poke up from the soil a few days later, I'm actually excited, which is honestly embarrassing. I can't believe that the kind of high I used to get from a chip upgrade is now provided by a leaf. All the same, it's weirdly fascinating to watch over the next few weeks as the stalk strengthens and gets taller, unfurling more tiny leaves. It's crazy that it came from the tiny little dead-looking thing I stuck in the soil.

I call him Chase. Chase the Chilli.

Michael catches me talking to Chase one day, which is how I know I'm actually going insane. He doesn't seem to think so, though, given how delighted he is. He shows me all the plants he's reared over the years and then helped plant outside, including some of the purple flowers I like. It turns out that they're called pansies and they're actually pretty easy to grow. He promises to get me some seedlings off the warden.

While Chase and his new friends—Posy, Pip and Percy, because I might as well embrace the insanity—are busy growing, Michael starts me on the third stage of the plan: making bread by hand.

It's the slowest, most involved process I could possibly imagine. I have no idea why anyone would ever actually do this willingly when they can buy it or use a machine to make it. Michael won't even let me use an old-fashioned stand mixer to knead the dough: I have to punch it and fold it myself.

Unsurprisingly, my first attempt goes badly; I end up with a brick of dense flour that even Michael doesn't dare to taste. I stare at it, looking extra pathetic next to Michael's perfectly shaped loaf, and find my hands shaking. A wave of fury sweeps over me. Why can't I do this right? Why can't I do the *simplest fucking things*? I shouldn't be stuck here like this, lower than the lowest people out there, stranded, listening to a fat, simple man babbling on about humanity and love and other shitty slogans. This isn't fair.

Before I can stop myself, I sweep everything—even Michael's bread—off the table and onto the floor. A glass bowl smashes into a thousand pieces and I'm viciously satisfied by the mess it makes. Without looking at Michael's face, I stalk out of the kitchen.

He finds me in the gardens, pacing up and down and still vibrating with anger. I turn on him, waiting for the clichéd words, for the pat on the shoulder—but he doesn't give them to me. Instead he sits down on a nearby bench, not looking at me.

"Do you want to know why I'm here?" he asks.

The question takes all the wind out of my sails. I've wondered about it a few times—of course I have. A person like Michael, with his pansies and homemade bread, doesn't belong here.

"Twenty years ago," he tells me, "I killed someone."

I stare at him. He's joking. There's no way he's not joking.

"I was addicted to a racer game—you know, those ones where you customise your own cars and take part in tournaments. I spent all my waking hours playing it. Spent thousands of pounds on it, too. My virtual world became everything to me. My family and friends stopped talking to me because of my obsession. It got so bad I couldn't focus on my job. I even played while I was driving my actual car. And one day I hit a teenager who'd run out after his football."

I don't know what to say.

"They think they know what humanity is, David," Michael says. "They think we've reached the pinnacle of evolution, now that limitations don't exist and technology and nature are blended so seamlessly you can't tell where one begins and the other ends. But they're wrong. We've forgotten the things that really make us human—the simple connections we make that mean more than any interaction we could have on the cybernet."

He gets up and stands there for a moment, still not looking at me.

"We'll try again tomorrow," he says finally, and then he leaves me in the gardens, trying to put the pieces of my new perspective together.

I'm sure I'm getting it wrong again at every stage. How accurate can scales really be? I can't even tell how much the dough has risen. But when Michael pulls two loaves out of the oven—his neatly shaped and mine an ugly, bulbous mass—I can't push down a strange pride. When I cut a slice and taste it, still warm, I can't believe that I made it with my own hands. I've never thought about bread before other than its calorific and nutritious value. I just ate whatever my macros needed and followed my suggested diet plan.

"Good food has a story," Michael tells me as he butters a slice of his own loaf. It's really good butter, not the fake vegan stuff, and it's melting into the bread as he spreads it. "It means something."

I remember when I was ten and the other kids in my class made a private group chat and refused to let me join. Mum didn't say much, but she brought me a homemade muffin, cinnamon-scented, still warm from the oven, with giant chunks of melted white chocolate and a crunchy, sugary topping. Tears come to my eyes, and I have to duck my head so that Michael can't see.

As I stare down at my bread, thinking of the sandwiches Mum used to make me for school, thinking of Ellen's pansy-purple curtains and how excited she was when we bought them, something falls into place. I feel like I'm finally beginning to grasp, if only dimly, what Michael has been trying to tell me.

There's a clink, and I look up to see that Michael has set a cup of tea beside me. He's remembered, as he always does, exactly how strong I like it. To my horror, that only makes the tears come faster. I try to wipe them away, but Michael puts his hand on my arm again.

"It's okay to cry," he says softly. "It's only human."

ACKNOWLEDGEMENTS_

Bright Neon Futures was conceived in very different circumstances than those we are faced with today. We wanted to put a fresh spin on a genre that is often portrayed as dark and dystopian, create something that would put a smile on someone's face. With all that came to pass in 2020, we doubted we would be able to publish this small passion project. Would people be interested in answering the call for submissions? Would they have the energy and time to write in times like these? Would *we* be able to put it all together?

The answer lies in your hands.

What was just a concept, a hope, became the very ethos behind this anthology. First and foremost, we are grateful to our authors. They gave their all to craft these stories, and went above and beyond what was expected of them. Thank you for being so responsive to feedback and communicating with us. Thank you for your words of support and encouragement. We hope you love *Bright Neon Futures* as much as we do and that you will proudly display it on your shelves many years to come.

Thank you to Luana, our cover artist, who took on our commission despite her incredibly busy schedule. We are grateful for the love and care you put into creating a cover that perfectly embodies the content of this anthology. We couldn't stop opening the file over and over again just to stare at it.

Lastly, we are grateful to each other. It was only the three of us running everything—from editing to publicity, production and distribution—and we wouldn't have been able to pull through without each other's support. We faced some very tough challenges in our private and professional lives, but we were able to manage all setbacks *together*. Our bonds are stronger because of it and we will look back on this project fondly.

We are immensely proud of *Bright Neon Futures* and of every single person who contributed to its realisation. It would have been impossible to publish it without you.

Thank you.

Ed, Angie, Hayley

Printed in Great Britain
by Amazon

17308599R00059